C000285642

MOORLAND MOUSIE

This edition is dedicated to the memory of
'Golden Gorse'

They called me 'Mousie'

MOORLAND MOUSIE

By
GOLDEN GORSE

Illustrations by
LIONEL EDWARDS

First Published, October 1929

This edition published 2011 by The Moorland Mousie Trust

Copyright
Text: © Estate of Muriel Wace
Illustrations © Estate of Lionel Edwards
ISBN 978 0 9570453 0 9

All rights reserved. No part of this publication may be reproduced, stored in a retrieval system, or transmitted, in any form or by any means, electronic, mechanical, photocopying, recording or otherwise, without the prior permission of the publishers.

This book is sold subject to the condition that it shall not, by way of trade or otherwise, be lent, resold, hired out, or otherwise circulated without the publisher's prior consent in any form of binding or cover other than that in which it is published and without a similar condition including this condition being imposed on the subsequent purchaser.

Typeset/design by Diana Lunn
Printed and bound by
Short Run Press Ltd. Exeter

Published and distributed by
The Moorland Mousie Trust
Exmoor Pony Centre
Ashwick . Dulverton
Somerset . TA22 9QE
Telephone: 01398 323093
email: info@exmoorponycentre.org.uk
www.moorlandmousietrust.org.uk

Acknowledgements

Thank you to all those who have helped me to realise the dream of reprinting Moorland Mousie.

My thanks to the estate of Golden Gorse for permission to use the story, and to Lionel Edward's estate for permission to use the illustrations.

To my husband Mike, for his continued support and encouragement; all trustees, past and present, in particular Sue Wingate and Juliet Rogers, who have travelled on the journey with me; Diana Lunn for finally getting the publication under way, and her family, David, Eleanor and Verity for their un-ending patience and help during the publication process.

Valerie Sherwin
June 2011

Written in 1929, this is a book of its time, exactly as it was written. Ponies pull the carts of tradesmen; long distances are covered by train, not horseboxes; fox and stag hunting is a part of life and their outcomes celebrated; and motors are the enemies of ponies – noisy and frightening.

CONTENTS

ILLUSTRATIONS

I was delighted to hear that one of my favourite childhood books, Moorland Mousie, was to be reprinted. This wonderful book brings back many happy memories of the hours my sister and I spent galloping over the moors with Moorland Mousie and his friends – inspired by the magical plates by Lionel Edwards.

Things have not always been so idyllic. Since the Second World War the Exmoor pony has become an endangered species and it is thanks to the tireless work of the Moorland Mousie Trust, of which I am proud Patron, that the Exmoor ponies still exist. Without the inspired work and commitment of the Trust we would not have this magnificent breed as part of our British heritage.

I hope that children today will love it as much as we did, and Mousie and his friends will enhance their lives, as they did ours.

Camilla

MOORLAND MOUSIE

CHAPTER I

I introduce myself and my Cousin Tinker Bell—My Pretty Mother—Tinker's Funny Ways—Happy Days on Exmoor—Kind Farmers—The Dog who went Sheep Killing—How the Red Deer sent Me about my Business—The Hind who would not let Us see her Calf—Our Neighbours on the Moor—Tinker Bell's Song—We see Hounds running and Determine to be Hunters Ourselves.

TINKER BELL and I were both born on Withypool Common in the same lovely month of May, and as I was only a day or two the elder I don't really remember at all what it was like without him. Everybody who knows Exmoor knows Withypool Common, and our special valley, between two steep hills, ran right down to the river bank where we used to drink. My Mother was very fond of this valley. She always lived there when she was alone apart from the herd, and Aunt used to go with her. Aunt was Tinker Bell's mother.

My Mother was dark brown with a mealy nose, just as if she had dipped it in a bucket of meal. "Regular Exmoor," I heard a farmer say once about that colouring. Aunt was quite different in colour, though much the same in shape. She was bright bay with black points, and she too had a mealy nose. Tinker Bell was just like her when he got older, but his first coat was a softer, more mousy colour.

Aunt, who was always rather sharp-tongued, used to tell me I wasn't half as good-looking as My Mother. I certainly didn't think my coat quite so pretty as hers; it was a mousy brown, a brown with some grey in it—and that is why they called me Mousie. My Mother was the most beautiful pony that ever was, and I never set up to be as good-looking as she was, but I was a very handsome pony all the same, and later on in my life I was immensely admired; every child who saw me used to say: "Oh! I wish I had a pony just like that!"

The first things I remember are My Mother's kind eyes and her soft wrinkled muzzle and snuggling close to her warm side. She would call

1

in a soft low whinny to me, encouraging me to walk a few steps to her. At first my legs felt all weak and tottery, but I soon got over this. Every hour I grew stronger, and in a day or two I was thoroughly busy and happy, exploring and making friends with everybody, including, of course, Tinker Bell. Tinker Bell was a very lively little fellow, and from the beginning he was funny! He was always talking, but fortunately he hadn't a sharp tongue like Aunt, and he was always capering about and doing something ridiculous. Such a pace he used to go on his long legs, trotting over the heather with a tremendous high action or galloping round and round with his fluffy tail, like a fox's brush, stuck straight out behind him.

I can see him now, after all these years, trotting round us very proud of a song he had just made:

> "Just a little pony
> In the month of May,
> Dancing in the heather
> All the day."

He used to sing this often as he careered about, until Aunt got very much annoyed and forbade him to sing it again in her presence.

"Then I'll sing it in her absence," said Tinker Bell to me in the impertinent way he had; and he made this the excuse for going further afield than he had before, and I went with him.

We had all sorts of wonderful adventures—wonderful to us, anyway, because everything was new and the world so very beautiful. Though I am an old pony now and have been to many places, I have never seen any more beautiful than Exmoor. The wide rolling hills of heather, grass, and bracken; the deep combes, each with its own enchanting busy little stream hurrying down to the lowlands; the huge, ancient oaks; the high sheltering beech-hedges—how much happiness we ponies got from them all. We loved the deep combes, heather-clad or with forests of stunted oak-trees, sometimes wreathed with honeysuckle. Then there were the wide cloud-scapes, and distant view of the Severn Sea, silver, blue and ever-changing. But perhaps the colour was the most wonderful thing of all—in the winter every shade of brown and grey, a beautiful harmony; in spring more brilliant browns and splashes of vivid green deepening through the summer months. In early autumn the moor was a sea of purple, as the heather and heaths came out, then a sudden change to gold of every shade, and yellows and browns; perhaps this was the most beautiful time of the year. Of course I didn't think of all this when I was a foal; but sometimes, later in my life, in the noisy dusty streets where I was so unhappy, a sudden memory would come over me, and I could see again the Exmoor hills as if I was there.

We made great friends with many of the sheep. Exmoor ponies and Exmoor sheep are generally seen together, and both are dear to every Exmoor farmer's heart, particularly the sheep, who are so defenceless. Later I often heard the farmers say: "The sheep have more enemies than any other animal"; and it always seemed to me that the farmers were fonder of their sheep than of any of the rest of their stock. It was terrible to see them tormented when the flies got bad in the autumn. The farmers were tireless in their attention at that time; they would come miles every day or two with their sheep-dogs, tie their horse up to a shady beech hedge, produce a large bottle of disinfectant from their pocket, and attend to all who needed care.

One farmer in particular we often watched from afar. One day My Mother remarked:

"Do you notice Farmer over yonder? He's got his best coat on—what a funny thing when he's come out to attend to the sheep! What do you think it means, children?"

But we could not guess.

"I dare say he told his wife that he was going to attend to the sheep," said Aunt; "but she knew well enough what was up when she saw him ride out of the yard in his best coat. He won't attend to them overlong today. Keep your eyes open, and before long you'll see hounds and Farmer with them." And it all fell out just as she said.

Hounds came into view on the far hill running hard. Most of the riders were a mile behind. Two people only were close to the hounds. One was the huntsman, and the other was Farmer. He was shouting out news of the stag, and thoroughly happy, and well he deserved to be.

How clever the sheep-dogs were, too! With their kind, brown eyes and shaggy coats they seemed only second to Farmer in their care of the sheep. They used to get very tired sometimes; they had to travel tremendous distances, and their lives were often shortened by the hard work they did. How different they were from that terrible dog we saw early one morning out on the moor chasing a terrified ewe among the heather; he got her down, when she was too tired to run any more, and killed her, and then he slunk home—a dog disgraced for ever.

Sometimes we saw the great Red Deer, the Kings of Exmoor. I was drinking one day from a dark peaty stream, and admiring my reflection—I felt sure that my forelock had grown an inch at least since I had last looked at it—when a big stag came stepping daintily along the grassy track. He was taller than a full-grown pony, and had such an array of great branching horns on his head that I felt quite scared. What a magnificent, noble animal he looked! He held his head so high and proudly, but when he stamped his foot and tossed his head and said fiercely:

"Don't you know this is my path! Move off, young man, and pretty quick too!" how I scurried!

Then one day we came across a hind, a beautiful, gentle-looking creature; she was busy with something in the bracken. We found out later it was her calf. She had just pushed it down into a mass of fern to have a sleep, and of course Tinker and I hurried up to see what it was she was doing. But we did not stay long! Her kind face suddenly changed to one of fury as she turned on us, and she said angrily to me:

"Don't come here, Mr. Impertinent; where are your manners?" And we both scuttled off as hard as we could lay legs to the ground. She would have knocked us down, I am sure, if we had delayed a single moment.

Sometimes we saw a fox with his ruddy coat, slipping through the fern and heather, much occupied with some deep-laid scheme of his own. He never stopped to talk, he was far too busy. How capable he looked!

"Well able to look after Number One," Aunt used to say as we watched him.

4

The mares and their foals were feeding apart

In the shallow water of the river we often saw a solitary fisherman, thin, tall, and grey. It was a heron. He would swallow fish after fish, but they never seemed to do him any good, and he remained just as thin and narrow as ever. He was a model fisherman, so patient and quiet. We liked to see him rise slowly from the water, spread his great grey wings, and flap steadily away, his thin legs straight out behind him. Away where the deep combes led down to the lowlands we saw the buzzards flying, one pair to each combe, sailing slowly round and round. But we liked the little birds the best of all—the stone-chats, chat-chatting, each on the top of his own furze-bush, and the friendly little meadow-pipits, who would run ahead of us as we grazed, taking a short flight every now and then.

By degrees we got to know Withypool Common pretty well. There were several herds of ponies, twelve or more in each herd. These ponies on the hill-side—bays, light browns and dark browns, occasionally a chestnut—made vivid splashes of colour. All were busy grazing; it is hard to pick up a living on Exmoor, and of animals cared for by man, only the sheep and the ponies can do it.

Some of the mares and their foals were feeding apart, but we never talked much. Of course we were specially interested in the little foals with their long legs, short bodies, furry coats, and fluffy tails, each in close attendance on his mother. We noticed that as they got older they began to go further away, and that was just like Tinker and me. What beautiful action they had, stepping so high over the heather; and how they could gallop when the mood seized them! But they would soon tire and would flop down for a rest in the heather, their legs stuck stiffly out before them, and their loving mothers brooding over them tenderly.

My Mother always stuck to her valley for headquarters, and it was the same with the others, they were always more or less to be found in the same places. Every day the world seemed to grow more beautiful; the sun was warmer, the whortleberries taller and greener, the heather began to show a brighter brown, the cotton-grass was more fluffy, warning us of the boggy places—and there were one or two very boggy places, not far from home. The little moorland flowers, Bog Asphodel, Sun-dew, and Ivy-leaved Campanula, came out one after the other, and Tinker Bell

The whole Hunt Streaming away towards Luttypool.

and I admired them all and tasted everything to see what was best.

That summer was perfection, and we enjoyed every minute of it.

Soon it was August, and the whole moor was turning purple; the scent of the heather was like honey, and the bees were crazy and tumbling about with excitement over the harvest they were gathering.

"We shall be seeing the hunters again soon," said My Mother; "when they come this way, children, you stick close to us and don't go losing your silly little heads."

The very next day, we were having our midday doze under My Mother's thorn tree when we heard them coming. The sound was thrilling, quite unlike any other. One deep note, then another, and then a whole chorus. First came the leading hound over the hill uttering his deep "ough, ough, ough!" Then came a long-drawn-out string of the rest of the pack, crying sometimes in chorus and sometimes alone.

Whether it was their voices or the sight of those huge hounds, as beautifully made as a horse, and all intent on one thing, I don't know, but we all of us were thrilled with excitement, and to this day I can never see hounds without a thrill going right through me. Down they came towards us, passing only a hundred yards away, and up the other side, going slowly, I thought, and yet they must have been going a good deal faster than they looked, because they were gone up that steep hillside in no time.

Round the top of our valley we saw the huntsman cantering steadily on a long-tailed thoroughbred horse, and then half a dozen more riders.

"Come on, children," said My Mother; "hurry on and we'll see some more of the fun."

She and Aunt galloped up to the head of the valley followed by us children, and there we saw the whole hunt streaming away towards Withypool.

Even Tinker Bell was speechless with astonishment. We didn't know that there were so many horses in the world—beautiful, well-bred horses, sailing along smoothly and easily, with their riders looking as if hunting was the easiest thing; and pulling horses, their riders exhausted and anxious, seeing downhill and rough going before them, and wondering whatever would happen now. There were farmers who knew all about it, and would almost certainly be in at the death, although to look at their out-of-condition mounts that would be quite impossible; nervous people going very steady; heavy-weights who were getting along as fast as circumstances permitted; and then the rag-tag and bob-tail who were having just as much fun as anybody else; fat cobs with beginners on them, little ponies with children, horses out of condition, horses just off the farm—there they went, all getting along as fast as ever they could go, and all determined that whatever happened they would not be left behind.

Our eyes devoured the scene until the last little pony, with stubby short legs, trotting as hard as he could go and ridden by a tiny girl—with a little black velvet jockey cap on—was out of sight.

Of course Tinker Bell was the first to speak.

"When I grow up," he said, "I shall be a hunter."

CHAPTER II

Autumn on Exmoor—The Fat Man in the Bog—Lorna comes over the Hill—Lorna and Flabber—How Flabber disobeyed her Father about the Crupper—Pride goes before a Fall—A Saddle slips on a Grass-fed Pony—Flabber lands on the Bank—Lorna finds herself her own Master.

AUGUST was nearly over, and the nights were getting cooler. In the daytime it was still very hot and the flies were "terrifying." My Mother knew where they were fewest, and she and Aunt knew just the best place for any particular time of day, so that we always kept moving on at definite intervals.

One late afternoon, we were resting under the shade of the little thorn tree, at the bottom of our special valley. My Mother was particularly fond of this spot; there was a bog there, and only she and Aunt and some of the Exmoor sheep knew how to cross it.

"I have seen some funny scenes, when the hunters came this way," she once said.

She turned to my Aunt: "Do you remember the day when that stout man who wore such bright-coloured clothes in front (I found out afterwards that the clothes a man wears in front are called 'waistcoats') forced his mare to cross the bog, though she knew better, poor dear, and tried hard not to, and they sank in up to her girths, and two or three men had to stay behind to get them out with ropes, and branches cut and laid down to make the ground firm?"

Hounds had been out that particular day of which I am talking. We knew it, but we had seen nothing of them. Suddenly My Mother threw up her head. She was gazing at the hill above us, and there, on the sky-line far away, we could see a pony, and hear her voice calling.

"Why," said My Mother, "I do declare it's Lorna!"

She sent a shrill cry back again, and Aunt joined in. The pony on the hill-top put down her head and came cantering steadily down the hill towards us. How well she moved. The hill was steep and rough, but she came down easily, as if the going was quite level.

My Mother was very pleased and kept tossing her head.

"Now children," she said, "you will hear all the news. Lorna used to live with us here, but I have not seen her for more than a year. She will have lots to tell us."

By this time the stranger pony had reached the bottom of the valley, and was picking her way over the short turf, which was so brilliant a green that wise ponies were warned that the ground was boggy.

What a pretty pony she was! She had the small distinguished head of the Exmoor, the short prick ears, and bright intelligent eyes. How alert and wide-awake she looked! She had little legs like a deer, and yet so strong that one could easily believe what My Mother often said, that an Exmoor would carry a big farmer for miles over the moor and never tire.

She came straight up to My Mother, and one soft muzzle gave greeting to the other.

"Well," she said, "I *have* had some fun today. When I've had something to eat I can tell you a tale that will make you all laugh."

She settled down to eat, and we waited patiently, longing to hear her news, but she went on eating steadily for a very long time, chuckling to herself at intervals.

At last she was finished and she joined us under our thorn tree. She and My Mother stood head to tail, flicking the flies from each other's heads, and we stood near by so as not to miss a word.

Lorna had obviously had a saddle on quite recently. We could see the saddle-mark still on her, and lines of sweat where the girths had been. Of course we knew all about saddles, for Mother and Aunt had told us.

"I've had such a time," Lorna began; "you know that fat girl, Flabber, who bought me last year—you saw her riding one day—well, I've taken a rise out of her all right!"

"Why? Didn't you like her?" said Tinker Bell eagerly.

"Of course I didn't," said Lorna. "How could I?"

"Wasn't she nice?" said I.

"Of course she wasn't," said Lorna, "or she wouldn't have been called Flabber. What silly children you are!"

"Be quiet, children," said Aunt. "We don't want to hear you talk. Go on please, Lorna."

"Well, it was like this," said Lorna. "I've always hated Flabber, specially since that day last year, but I'll tell you that another time, and today I got a bit of my own back. You know Flabber is fat and heavy; she eats too many sweets and she won't take the trouble to keep in condition, and she has always been too full of herself to think about me. She likes people to say she rides well, and what pretty hair she's got, and she likes to be comfortable, but she never bothers whether I'm comfortable or not. Well, this morning there was a meet at Exford, and Flabber was going. Her father was away, but she was to go alone. She rides quite well for her age, but of course she will never be first class. When she came round to the stable, I was bridled and saddled waiting for her.

" 'Oh, Tom,' she said to the groom, 'you'd better take that crupper off, the pony can quite well do without it now.'

" 'I don't think so, Miss,' said Tom. 'She's still fat; she's only on grass; when she has galloped a bit and sweated herself down she'll be smaller, the saddle will go right on to her shoulders, and then she'll start pulling, and maybe she'll fall down, with the weight forward like that. The master said I was always to put it on if she needed it.'

"Now there had been trouble about this crupper before. Flabber didn't like it, because she wanted to look grand and grown-up, and none of the big hunters wore one. She knew quite enough about riding to know that a crupper kept a saddle well back in its right place, but she thought that she would do without it and girth me a little tighter, and so make the saddle keep back. She knew that ponies hate being girthed tight, but she didn't care; that is Flabber all over.

"Well, they went on talking, and at last she persuaded Tom to take the crupper off. It was only five miles to the meet, and we trotted along steadily and got there easily within an hour. We found our stag quite quickly, and scent seemed good, and we were soon galloping hard over the shoulder of Dunkery. Now Flabber had tightened my girths soon after starting, but she had forgotten to do so again, because she had happened to fall in with a friend and their tongues had never ceased—and you know a grass-fed pony without a crupper needs very careful girthing indeed.

"Well, I was galloping all out, and, as you know, I'm very fast. I was

We found our Stag quite quickly —

thoroughly enjoying myself. The going was perfection, and it was not too hot. But after a bit I began to feel that saddle slipping. We had left Stoke Pero on our right, then it was all down hill, but there was no time to stop now. Hounds were running hard; their voices chimed up from the valley below. The pollen from the heather flew in clouds as we brushed through it. The sea shone away on our right, the cool wind blew. The great hunters were galloping in front, behind, and around me; I was not going to be last, not I!

"At this moment Flabber became conscious that the saddle was slipping. She tried to pull me up, but the saddle was so far forward that all her weight was in front, and it would have been hard to stop even if I had wanted to. Of course, as you know, I have a lovely mouth, but when all the weight gets forward on a down hill, what can one do?

"I was far too excited to study Flabber's comfort just then, and on I went. The path got very narrow and very steep—we were going down to Nutscale Water. I became aware that things were getting serious. We were still cantering, and everybody was pushing and scrambling down the narrow path, some because they wanted to get on, and some because they couldn't stop their mounts. The saddle was slipping at every stride. Flabber was getting agitated. I could feel that; but we were only half-way down, and when we saw some of the field tearing up the opposite side, we all got more excited than ever.

"The saddle was now pushing right at my elbows and coming over my neck. Flabber made a desperate effort to stop me, but I couldn't stop. It was too late!

"The great horse in front was pulling hard, his rider was trying to steady him. Flabber couldn't steady me, and I ran into his hind quarters. The saddle gave another lurch forward, and Flabber scrambled off on the bank, the best thing she could do in the circumstances. The great horse went on, and I after him.

"A man behind called out, 'I'll catch the pony when we get to the bottom.' 'Will you?' thought I!

"We were down at last; the saddle slipped back a bit. The horses were crossing the brook and going straight up the other side, but I turned sharp right-handed. There was a sheep track, just right for me, and I knew no big horse would care to follow me along that narrow path. I galloped off half a mile; first one stirrup flew off, and then another. What cared I! I left them lying in the heather. I could hear the hounds chiming away on my left. I bucked myself right out of the saddle, as I went down a steep little pitch, and I was free!

"I could hear no more now. All was absolutely still. One lazy bee buzzed in the heather. I rubbed my bridle off, had a good roll and a drink. How nice it was without Flabber! What a peaceful, happy spot!

"I was my own master! Nutscale Water is a lovely place! Such a delicate flavour the heather has, and the bracken tops were just right, and I found the loveliest bit of grass. I had a topping time. And then I came along to see you. I had to come by Lanacre, so as to avoid Exford. They would have stopped me there."

"And what happened to Flabber?" said Tinker Bell.

"Walked home," chuckled Lorna.

"How far?" said My Mother.

"Seven miles," said Lorna.

"Had she top-boots on?" said Aunt.

"She had," said Lorna.

"What difference does that make?" said Tinker Bell.

"Sore heels," chuckled Aunt.

She would tell us no more, though there were a hundred questions we wanted to ask. She wanted a good meal, she said. It was no good asking, perhaps she would tell us more tomorrow. My Mother led us up the combe to the hill-top, to a new grazing place, and we gradually worked our way on to another sheltered combe, our usual sleeping-place, and there we dozed standing.

At daybreak Tinker Bell was ready with a question.

"Why do you hate Flabber?" he asked Lorna.

"Be quiet," said Aunt.

"Never ask questions until your elders have had breakfast," said My Mother.

After breakfast Tinker tried again.

"Why...?" he began.

"Be quiet," said Aunt, "we are going to sleep now."

The sun was now well up and warm, and we ponies lay down on the warm hill-side for an hour's real rest.

CHAPTER III

Why Lorna hated Flabber—A Selfish Rider—The Run of Lorna's Life—The only Pony at the Kill—Flabber accepts a Lift and Leaves Lorna behind—The Horrible Stable—A Night of Agony—The Terrors of Thirst—Morning at Last—Tom to the Rescue—Flabber has to do without Hunting.

LORNA got up and stretched herself. She raised her crest very high, drew in her nose till it touched her chest, stretched one hind leg out behind her and then the other.

She looked very distinguished, we thought, and very odd; we had never seen a pony do that before.

"I will tell you why I hate Flabber," she said.

"Why do you call her Flabber?" said Tinker.

"Because it suits her," said Lorna.

Tinker and I were all ears for this story, but it was no good being impatient. She put down her head and began to graze again.

For five minutes we waited, not daring to speak; not a sound could be heard but the regular tearing of the short grass and a steady munching. She then went up to My Mother and began to gnaw her mane vigorously. My Mother thoroughly enjoyed this and did the same for Lorna in return. At last, when they had quite finished, she moved off to the shade of the thorn tree, stood switching her tail slowly to and fro, and began:

"I told you yesterday that Flabber was quite a fair rider. She has ridden all her life, but she will never be first rate because she has no sympathy for her horse. She does not understand us, and so she will never get the best we have to give. She puts herself first; she is selfish and conceited.

"Last year in September we had a very good run. We ran from just above Porlock to quite near to Challacombe. I was in hard condition. I had been having three pounds of oats daily for the last two months, and I was ready to run for my life. There was a delicious scent of falling leaves as we started. On the moor the bracken was all golden; the purple heather was quite over. I flung the black peaty soil behind me, as we raced down to Badgery Water. I scampered up Hoccombe Water, across the road at Brendon Two Gates, down into one combe, up the other side,

17

gaining on the big horses at the steepest down hills, getting a bit behind up hill, getting a bit forward again where the going was worst; and at last we killed our deer not far from Challacombe.

"I was the only pony there, and two or three people came up to Flabber and said how well she had ridden and what a good pony she had, and Flabber smiled and looked pretty—she was always good at that. It was a long way home, and to tell the truth I was, for the first time in my life, a little bit tired. Flabber is no light weight, and what's more, she is always soft and out of condition, and rides twice as heavy as she ought to—too fond of sweets, and doesn't take enough exercise.

"Still I was willing and ready to trot the 14 miles home across the moor as gaily as could be. Flabber was very thirsty, and seeing an inn close at hand, and having a sixpence in her pocket, she went to ask for a glass of ginger-beer.

"She didn't ask for a drink for me. I knew my Flabber, but I did think that when I stopped at the little stream by the road, and asked to be allowed to drink, she might have spared the time. After all, it was I who had done all the work.

"Well, she drank her ginger-beer, and I knew how much she felt refreshed by the contented sigh she gave. A long gallop is thirsty work.

"By that time the field had dispersed in different directions, and Flabber paid for her drink and turned for home. She was a bit out of her usual country, and was just about to ask her way when a motor drew up.

" 'Hello!' said the man driving, whom I recognised as a neighbour of ours. 'What a long way from home you are. Can't I give you a lift?'

" 'I should love it,' said Flabber. 'We've had a tremendous gallop. But what about the pony?'

" 'Oh, she'll be all right; leave her at the inn and let your groom fetch her.'

"Flabber thought a minute. She had orders from her father never to leave her mount at an unknown stable if she could possibly help it, and always to get home quietly after hunting as soon as possible. But her father was away, and her mother spoilt her. She thought she might risk it.

" 'Would you wait two minutes, and I'll come,' she said.

Killed or died not far from Mullacomba

"She enquired at the inn. Yes, they had a stable, said the girl, but the man was away, and they didn't generally put up horses.

" 'Oh, this pony's very quiet,' said Flabber. 'She'll be all right anywhere. Just ask the man to feed her, and we'll send for her in an hour or two.'

"The girl obviously knew nothing about ponies, but she opened the stable door, and Flabber led me in.

"It was a horrid stable—no horse had been in it for years. It smelt of chickens and dust, there were empty wine bottles all about, and the nasty smell of petrol. Flabber found a mass of musty hay; she put down an armful in front of me, but even she must have known it was not fit to eat.

"She found an old broken halter and tied me to the manger. She never even loosed my girths, which were very tight.

" 'Tell the man to feed the pony when he comes in,' she said to the girl, and she slammed the door and went off.

"I could hear her talking cheerfully to her friends. They were rather grand people, and Flabber liked them like that. Then the motor went off. I didn't worry much at first, I was expecting the man to come any moment. He would be like Tom, I thought, and would loosen my girths and shift the saddle on my back, and rub me down, and give me some gruel and a bit of sweet hay, and I should be all right until I was sent for. Perhaps, even, he would turn me out in that nice field, and let me have a roll, and dry myself in the beautiful fresh air.

"But nobody came. I had been sweating a good deal when I was put in. Standing tied up like that, there was no chance of getting dry, and I began to feel cold and started to shake. How often I had heard Flabber's father say: 'Never leave your pony until she is comfortable, dry, and warm.'

"But there was something worse still than the wet and cold: my body was beginning to swell, and those girths cut into me, as if every minute someone was drawing them tighter. And then, worst of all, I was so terribly, terribly thirsty. As for food, I could not have eaten anything, I was feeling too bad.

"The man never came, and it began to get dark. Every minute seemed to increase my sufferings. I did not know that there could be anyone in

20

the world in so much pain and so unhappy and miserable as I was.

"Then I think I got light-headed, because I remember nothing more of that awful night, nor of the coming of the morning. The next thing I knew was Tom's soft Devonshire voice saying: 'Poor little pony! Poor little pony!'

"He was unbuckling my girths, and taking off my bridle. It was all I could do to stand. I don't think I should have lived much longer; but how good it was to know that Tom was there. I knew he would do everything he could for me. He went off to the inn and got me some gruel, but I was too weak to drink more than a mouthful. He went away then and found a juicy apple in the orchard. He knew I loved them, and I was able to take a bite, then a handful of fresh grass, and then another sip of gruel, and gradually I got a little stronger.

"I just managed to walk out of the stable, and he led me into the orchard, and after a little coaxing I ate a little more grass and felt a bit better. The day was very still and sunny. How thankful I was to be out of that horrible prison, where I had made sure that I should die!

" 'You wait here, Lorna,' said Tom. 'I am going to find you real good quarters; you are too weak to get home today.'

"He was back in an hour. I was feeling better and was doing a little grazing on my own account.

" 'You'll soon be in clover little one,' he said; 'you come along.' He led me off a mile down the road, and it was all I could do to get so far; and then we came to Farmer Rawle's, who had promised to care for me until I was stronger. There was a lovely sheltered shed, with water in it, and a grass field and trees and everything one could want. Farmer Rawle promised to look after me.

" 'She will be better out,' he said. 'These Exmoors always do better at grass. She won't be fit to get back to your place for another week at least. If it was my girl, I'd give her a tanning.'

"No one could have been kinder to me than Farmer was, and in a fortnight's time I was able to get back home. It was long before I heard the full story of Flabber's iniquity. She had apparently gone home with her friends, had tea with them on the way, and then they had motored her back the last mile or two. Her father was coming back that night, and

Tom had gone to fetch him in the motor. He would not be back until late.

"Flabber was in bed and asleep when the Captain and Tom got back, but Mrs. Hurst told them that I was all right. Flabber had left me at 'The Nine Bells'; she had given orders about me, and said the stable was a good one.

"The Captain was not quite satisfied, and before breakfast next morning he gave Tom orders to ride over at once and fetch me home.

"When Tom got back later I heard there was a terrible scene, and the Captain told his daughter that he was ashamed of her.

"Flabber made excuses and said she 'never thought.'

" 'I have told you before,' said the Captain, 'that more harm is done in this world by want of thought than in any other way, and this is especially true of animals. Those who neglect their animals have no right to have any. I am ashamed to have a daughter who could behave like that.'

"Well, I got my strength back by degrees, but I heard Tom say that a horse would have been ruined for life by such treatment; only a pony would get over it.

"Flabber missed her hunting all last winter, and it was not till the spring came that I was considered strong enough to carry her again."

Lorna finished her story and began to graze again.

Tinker Bell's eyes were wide with fright.

"But I thought human beings were so nice," said he.

"Some of them," said My Mother.

CHAPTER IV

Lorna describes the Horse Show—My Mother's Poem—Tom comes to fetch Lorna Away—Good-bye, good-bye!

LORNA stayed with us three days, and we enjoyed listening to her tales. She had been about so much and she seemed to know everything.

One evening she was telling us about the farmers' luncheon at Exford Horse Show. "I was there," she said, "tied up outside, and I could hear everything. They said a lot of interesting things, but what I liked best was something the Master quoted in his speech. He said it was written by Charles Kingsley. It describes the end of a stag-hunt, and I thought it was lovely—just what I feel myself: 'The blowing of the Morte, the last wild holloa, when the horn notes rang through the autumn woods and rolled up smooth flat mountain sides; and Brendon answered Countisbury, and Countisbury sent it on to Lynmouth Hills, till it swept out of the gorge and died away upon the Severn Sea.' "

"That's nice!" said Aunt; "just like it; and I know all those places."

"Is that poetry?" said Tinker Bell.

"No, silly!" said I. "Poetry is what My Mother sings us."

"What's that?" said Lorna.

"Oh, just something she heard them singing once when she was standing below Hawkridge Church. Please tell her, Mother!"

My Mother began to hum very softly:

> "All things bright and beautiful,
> All creatures great and small,
> All things wise and wonderful,
> The Lord God made them all.
>
> "The hunter in his stable,
> The pony on the moor,
> The little foal beside her,
> He made them, rich and poor."

"That's not right!" said Aunt; "it doesn't go like that."

"That's what they were singing," said My Mother firmly.

*   *   *   *

On the third day after Lorna came, we were all standing under our favourite thorn tree when a horseman appeared far away on the hill above us.

"That's Tom," said Lorna, "and he's riding Starling, and he's come to fetch me."

"The horseman had seen us; he turned his horse and came steadily down the sheep track towards us. Lorna threw up her head and watched.

"I love Tom." she said.

When he got quite near, he got off his horse. He put his hand in his pocket, pulled out some oats, and called "Co'p! Co'p! my Pretty!"

"We'd best be going," said My Mother, and she and Aunt trotted off to a safe distance with us following. But Lorna stood quite still.

"Come, my Pretty!" called Tom, holding out his hand, and Lorna walked right up to him and put her nose into his hand.

"You'd best be coming home-along now," he said, and he slipped a halter very gently over her head, mounted his horse, and off they all went together up the hill.

"Good-bye! Good-bye!" cried Lorna to us.

"Good-bye!" we answered. "Come back soon!" And that was the last we saw of Lorna.

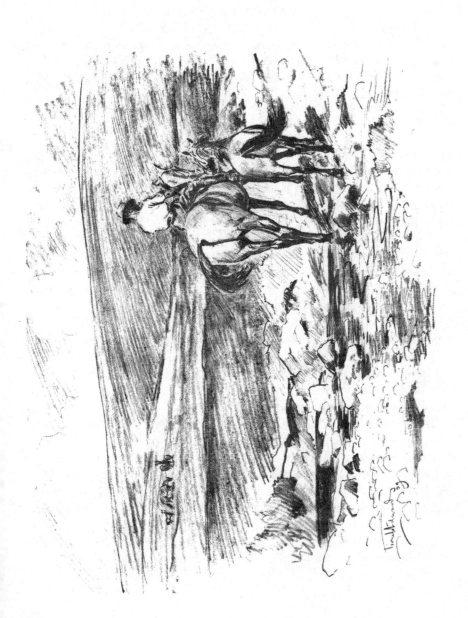

you'd best be coming along now

CHAPTER V

Good Times will not Last—The Farmers come to fetch us Away—My Mother and Aunt try to Save Us—The Three Farmers give Chase—My Mother's Plans are foiled—They Drive us into the Farmyard—We are Separated from Our Mothers—We see Cats for the First Time—And Smell a Farmer's Coat—The Old Brown Pony gives us no Sympathy—We Travel by Train and have our First Sight of Patience—Homesick Ponies.

TINKER and I had a very happy summer. The elders warned us that the good times would not last, but young people never really believe these warnings. The elders had said, more than once: "Winter is coming! Hard times are ahead! The moor will change, cold winds will blow, the sun will lose his warmth, the rain will soak through your coats, the goodness will go out of the grass, you will become as thin as rakes and very different little ponies from what you are now!" They told us tales of hard times on Exmoor, when bad winters came, and there was nothing to eat, and it was hopeless for hungry ponies to go round the farms begging for a mouthful of hay, because the farmers had not enough for their own stock, let alone the wild ponies. At such times yearlings and two-year-olds suffer the most, because they have no condition to fall back upon like the older ponies, and some even die from hunger and weakness. Aunt, who always took a melancholy view of things, once even said: "Someone will come to take you off the moor, and it will be a toss-up whether you get a good home or a bad one."

Tinker and I listened, but we did not really believe.

October was a glorious month, and though the sun was losing its heat our coats were getting longer every day, so it did not matter much. It was not likely that things would be as bad as the elders prophesied. We had heard them say old people generally get a bit crabbed, and their prophesies needed taking with a grain of salt. Aunt and Mother might not be really old, but perhaps they were old enough for that.

One day towards the end of October My Mother was humming over one of the poems she was fond of:

"Autumn gold, Autumn red,
Underfoot, overhead,
Gold-brown bracken for carpet rare
Rose-red berries for fairies' fare."

She was bothered because she couldn't remember how it went on, and she appealed to Aunt, but Aunt only said that she "didn't believe in poetry."

Of a sudden My Mother threw up her head; her eyes were fixed on the hill opposite to us, and following her gaze we saw a figure on horseback. At the same time we became aware of another horseman, not so far away either, coming over the hill behind us. My Mother moved uneasily a few paces up the valley, and then, viewing a third horseman on the left at the entrance of our valley, she called to us in an agony of apprehension:

"Quick, children, follow me!"

There was only one way open to us and that led up the valley. My Mother and Aunt went first, and Tinker Bell and I dashed after them. It really was rather fun, such a race and scramble; never had we seen the elders going so fast before, in and out the heather, round the stunted May trees, through the golden bracken, skirting the treacherous grass-green patches of bog, jumping the little brown streams—why, it was almost as good as hunting. Just at first I thought we had shaken off those three riders. We had left them behind, anyhow; but suddenly there they were again, one to the right, one to the left, and one behind us. Tinker and I didn't quite like this, we had thought it would be so easy to shake them off, and we began to get a little anxious and lose our self-confidence.

We were galloping now over rough hummocky bog, and our pursuers were on firmer ground to right and left of us. They were going at their ease, whilst we were tiring in the heavy going.

We came at last to a high bank which skirted a huge allotment where Exmoor stud-book ponies were kept, and we galloped on with this on our right. Suddenly My Mother called out:

"Don't go into the lane! Remember the lane!"

Then we saw the opening of the lane which ran down through the fence on our right, just ahead of us. We meant to dash past it on to the open moor beyond, but one of the riders on a fast long-legged horse was before us, cracking his whip, so that all my courage seemed to ooze away. We hesitated a moment, wondering which way to go, and then, before we had time to think, our enemies were on us, one behind, one at each side. There was only one way to go, and that was down the lane.

Down it we went pell-mell, and what a clattering our hooves did make. The men were now close behind us, red-faced, shouting, and furious they seemed to me.

"Keep them going," said one; "don't let them stop!"

On we dashed, full gallop. Half a mile further on the lane led into a road, and there Mother remembered there was a choice of turnings, and well she knew which one she should take. But alas! when we arrived at it, there was another horseman, cracking a huge whip and standing right in our way, and we were forced to take the turn which led away from the moor.

We were now going right away from home, and at every turning that we wanted to take, there by some magic was a farmer mounted on a great horse and cracking an enormous whip.

Tinker and I were now really terrified.

My Mother and Aunt spoke at intervals.

"Keep close, children," they said, "we'll save you yet"; and we knew that they had their eyes open for any weak place in the hedge, through which they could force their way.

Later on My Mother said:

"Don't worry, darlings, they're not half as bad as they look."

We had come four miles from the moor, and suddenly straight ahead we saw a snug-looking farmyard, with stacks of straw and hay, the first farm we had ever seen. In we dashed, through one gate, then another, and suddenly found ourselves prisoners in a big farmyard. Up came the four riders. One of them was saying:

"Got them pretty easily that time!"

"Yes," said the other. "We didn't give the mares time to think today. We'd best cut them out at once. I'm going home-along and will drive

them back to the moor."

One man got off his horse and came into the yard. He cracked his whip and came so near that we nearly died of terror. Suddenly I spied the gate open, and My Mother and Aunt dashing through it. Tinker Bell and I fled after them, but a whip cracked in our faces, the gate was banged, and we were left alone—prisoners!

"Come in and have a drink," said the farmer; and they all went off.

I have had many awful moments in my life, but I sometimes think this was the worst. I was dependent for everything on My Mother. I little knew how I loved her until then. Tinker and I stood in the corner of the yard petrified. There were so many terrible things around us. There were those great farm-buildings—we had never seen any buildings near at hand before; there was a coat hanging on the gate, giving out a most peculiar smell; there was the farmer's wife going through the yard to milk the cows; a savage-looking dog and three striped, long, thin animals which we found out were called cats at her heels; and there was a tiny child hanging over the wall and saying:

"Oh, look at the pretty little ponies!"

Each one of these was more terrifying than the last.

A brown head looked over the stable door; obviously it belonged to an old pony. We went up seeking for comfort.

"Silly little fools!" was all he said; but to see him so calm in the midst of everything did make one feel a trifle better.

I do not want to dwell on what happened next day. Each moment seemed more awful than the last. We were taken down to the station, the old pony trotting along in front, and before we knew what was happening we found ourselves shut into a horse-box on a train. We were weak now, or they would not have managed it so easily. We had had nothing to eat for ever so long. The farmer had put down a bundle of hay for us the night before, but we had no heart either to eat or drink.

Tinker Bell declared at intervals that he was going to die.

Two terrible hours of railway journey and we reached our destination. A small face looked in at the little doorway of the horse-box and a soft voice said:

"Hello, darlings! Have you arrived?"

30

This was my first sight of Patience, to whom I owe so much; but at that time I thought she was scarcely less frightful than the other human beings I had met. She was just ten years old; her brown plaits hung one over each shoulder, and it was not long before I grew to love her round, cheerful face. We were taken along the road to our new home, Patience on an old pony in front to give us a lead; our new owner, Colonel Coke, behind; and the Irish groom, Murphy, whom later I was to get very fond of, going ahead to see we did not bolt down the wrong turns.

Two very chastened little ponies arrived at Wootten, our new home. We were turned at once into a big grass field. We were tired, hungry, and dreadfully thirsty, but it was hours before we felt sufficiently recovered to try and graze, or to drink at the little pond.

Everything was so strange, so unlike home, and we had been through so much since we left the moor. The huge trees, the great hedges, the warm, still air, how different it all was!

CHAPTER VI

Patience begins to make Friends with Us—Tinker inspects the Pig Trough—We Become a little Bolder—We take Hay from Patience's Hand—Step by Step she makes us Tame—We are Happy at Wootten—Patience leads us about—Michael Takes a Hand—Tinker Steals Michael's Hat—Tinker and I give the Fat Sow a Lesson—My Adventure and Discovery.

THE next morning Patience came down to have a look at us. She climbed on to the gate and called, but we, of course, were terrified. Our experience of mankind till now had been horrible, and to us she seemed just one of the same species, and we fled to the very end of our pasture. Colonel Coke came later.

"Poor little creatures!" he said; "they do look miserable. You will have to tame them, Patience, as you did your robin; we shall do nothing with them until they have lost all that nervousness. You must feed them regularly each morning, give them a small bundle of hay and a few oats; they will soon begin to look for your coming."

Murphy came later and put down an iron pig trough in our field. How funny Tinker was about it; he went up to it when Murphy had gone, and very gingerly touched it with his nose. He had the square, sensitive, upper lip of the Exmoor, and he would stretch it out and use it for investigating everything as if it were a miniature elephant's trunk. The cold iron made him jump back a yard, and this made me smile for the first time since I had left My Mother.

Next morning Patience came again. She had a bundle of hay under her arm, and she was carrying a sieve in which were oats and chaff. The minute we saw her we fled; but later on when she had quite gone we came very cautiously up to the pig trough, where she had put the hay, and Tinker ventured to seize a mouthful. I hardly dared touch it myself, but I couldn't bear to let him have it all, and I very gingerly grabbed a tiny whisp. It was very good; there was no doubt about it; and in spite of our nervousness we were not long before we had finished it.

Later in the day we discovered the oats in the trough. How delicious they were! We had never tasted anything so good. The next morning Patience came again, and exactly the same thing happened; and so it

32

went on every day regularly. And every day we became a little bolder, and delayed less before we ventured up to our little manger.

After a bit we got so bold that we began to advance directly she came into the field, but of course we could not go right up to our manger until she had quite gone away.

At last we got really brave, and we did not mind eating while she hung over the gate and watched us.

"They're getting better," said Colonel Coke one day when he came with Patience to have a look at us "You'll have them feeding out of your hand before long."

The weather got colder, and when the grass lost its goodness, the hay and oats became more acceptable than ever.

Each day, in her little brown coat well buttoned up to her neck, and showing all her nice white teeth in a kind smile, Patience stood a little nearer as we fed. Of course we never took our eyes off her for one second, but we began to think that perhaps she wasn't quite as bad as the rest of them. At last she stood close up to the manger while we ate. A week of this and we began to lose our fear of her. One day there did not seem to be quite so much to eat as usual. Patience had been standing very quiet close up to the manger the whole time we ate, and when we finished we realized that she was holding out a tempting lock of hay. Tinker made a grab at it and we both fled; but after a bit I ventured to come back and grabbed a bit for myself. Each day we grew bolder, so that at last we would eat the whole of our feed bit by bit drawn from the bundle beneath her arm. Then we actually found we could venture to take oats out of her hand. She was very slow moving, and that is what gives ponies confidence; but when we first came to Wootten we should not have believed it if somebody had told us that we should ever become as bold as this.

From now on life became pleasanter. Fear is a terrible thing, and it is the greatest trouble of all horses. It was a wonderful thing to feel that there was at least one human being of whom we were no longer afraid.

By Christmas Patience had succeeded in getting us both haltered, and that without scaring us one little bit. She did it all step by step, making a tiny bit of progress each day—never impatient, never in a hurry—and it was not till a very long time after, when I had met all sorts of human beings and realized how little they understand horses and how impatient they are, that I realized what a wonderful child she was.

Colonel Coke said to a friend who came out with him one day to watch her that she had learnt it from taming her birds. She had a robin who hopped into the schoolroom for crumbs, and a tame canary, who sat on her finger and sang at the top of his voice.

Directly we were tame, we were ever so much happier. Instead of longing for the moor, we began to feel that we really were rather lucky to be so snug and well-fed now the cold weather had come. It was a pretty place, Wootten, all covered with creepers, long and low. We could see the house from our field, and we spent a great deal of time watching the people moving about, and wondering what they were really like and what the house was like inside, and whether anyone would come out and give us a tit-bit.

Soon after we had been haltered Patience began to lead us about, and so we got to know all sorts of interesting things, and every day we got bolder.

Sometimes Michael would come and lead Tinker, while Patience led me. Michael was only eight; he was Patience's brother; he had red hair and was very cheerful, and we soon got very fond of him too. He was always wanting to get on to Tinker, and it was all Patience could do to stop him. There was a smaller child Jack, but we didn't see much of him; he used to come and stand on the gate and talk to us, but he didn't come into the field. He was a very little fellow five years old, and I think he was a bit nervous.

Spring came and Wootten got prettier every day. Directly the grass began to grow Tinker and I started growing too. Then what a happy summer we had! The children were always in our field and we had great fun together. The first hot day, when Michael wore a big straw hat, Tinker would insist on biting it to see what it was made of. And then, I don't know how it was, but he seemed as if he couldn't open his mouth to let it go. Anyway, he pulled it off Michael's head, and then it flapped and frightened him, and off he went round the field with the big hat flapping in his mouth, looking just like Rover the big retriever dog, who

34

was always carrying sticks about. Michael was delighted, but Patience said the hat was new and she was afraid Tinker would spoil it—and he certainly did not do it much good!

Then there were the farm animals—the cows, the geese, the ducks, and the pigs—what fun we had with them! Murphy put down a lot of mangolds one day for us, and the old sow would eat more than her share.

"I'll teach her," said Tinker, and let fly with both heels at her fat sides. I did the same from the other side—I'm afraid we were both naughty ponies—and we sent the old lady grunting and scuttling off into the farmyard.

We had no shoes on, and of course we didn't really hurt her.

Our life was ideal. Time went on, one peaceful, happy day much like the last. Another year went by, and we were now big ponies, just three years old.

Soon after my third birthday I managed to do what I had been wanting to for a long time—I got right into the house. Patience had taken me up to the back door to talk to cook. I was very tame by now, and the more I saw of human beings the more I liked them. Patience left me at the door a moment while she went through to ask cook for a lump of sugar. I saw my opportunity and walked into the scullery after her. The scullery was narrow and I was rather fat, and when Patience opened the kitchen door, there I was just outside it, taking up the whole scullery, with no room to turn.

I hadn't learnt to back then, and cook got agitated; she didn't like seeing me blocking up the whole of her scullery, and eventually Patience said that the only thing to do was to take me through the kitchen, through the hall, and out at the front door. She held out a lump of sugar to encourage me; but I really would have gone without, I was so much interested, and it was all quite simple; but when Tinker Bell saw my head looking out at the front door, his eyes nearly dropped out of his head. He had often wanted to get into the house himself, but he had never managed it.

CHAPTER VII

*We Go to School with the Horse Breaker—We Learn to Trot in a Circle—and
then to Canter—Young Jem mounts Me for the First Time—The Terrors of
Traffic and the Virtue of Making Haste Slowly—Young Jem Disobeys his Father
and Ends in a Ditch—The Terrible Motor.*

IT was soon after this that Colonel Coke decided that it was time for us
to be broken in. It was autumn again, and we were now three and a half
years old. Patience *was* excited about it. She had ridden the old pony
that was used for the mowing machine quite a lot, and she was longing to
have a real good pony of her very own.

The breaker was an active little man, with very thin legs and a blue
spotted necktie, who lived some ten miles off. He had a great reputation
for carefulness and kindness. He arrived one morning on his cob, and
his son—who was something between a big boy and a young man—with
him. He seemed quite pleased with our appearance—"a good-looking
couple," he said. But he was specially pleased when he saw Patience
come up to us and halter us.

"I can see," he said, "that my work has been half-done. I don't as a
rule much care," he went on to the Colonel "about breaking in these
Exmoors, they come to me so wild; and people don't understand that
when they are like that, they need double the time to break if I am to
make a good job of them. I cannot do anything with them until they lose
their nervousness; but these ponies of yours are a different matter, and I
don't think we should have any trouble."

Well, he found we were quiet enough, and he led me off beside his
cob, while Tinker followed with his boy.

We were very lucky in Old Jem; he understood horses, and knew just
how to make them understand him, and Tinker and I quite enjoyed our
breaking in. We had always been a little jealous of horses who worked;
they seemed so knowledgeable, and we wanted to be like them.

Every day at Old Jem's we learnt something fresh. He kept us in a
dear little field, and twice a day for half an hour he would give us a
lesson.

36

I quite expect an interesting in.

First there was lunging, and that did need some understanding. I had a leather halter on and a long rope fixed to it, and Old Jem held it at one end, and Young Jem led me round and round in a a circle. After a bit I found out what they wanted me to do, and then I went round alone, and later on I learnt to trot on the circle and then to canter. Old Jem was always slow and steady; he didn't believe in hurrying us.

Next I learnt a very hard lesson—how to be tied up without trying to break my halter; and then how to carry a saddle, and bear the girths being tightened; and how to have a bridle in my mouth.

He taught me just as Patience had done, one thing at a time, and I progressed every day.

At the end of a month Young Jem got on me. I wasn't frightened of him, so I made no fuss at all, and he rode me daily round the fields, turning about in all directions, until I got quite handy.

Right from the beginning they had been leading me out on the road to get used to the traffic, and the things we saw were so terrible that it needed all the encouragement Old Jem could give to keep me from bolting home. I trusted him more than I trusted Young Jem, who was always a little bit hasty. He never quite believed what his father said—"more haste less speed." Old Jem would say to him:

"Never let the ponies get a fright, you can't force them into it"; but Young Jem was for speeding things up a bit and making his fortune quickly.

One day, just a week or two before we were to go back to Wootten, "quiet to ride," Young Jem put the saddle on me. He was going to take me down the road to get me more accustomed to heavy traffic. He knew well how it alarmed me, because when I passed a big lorry, I could never help trembling; but he thought it was high time I gave that up. He didn't believe what Old Jem said—"you can't force them into it"—and he decided to take me into the narrow station road, where big lorries were sure to come along. The first one that came, passed so close that I couldn't bear it. It seemed coming straight at me, and, just as I was alongside, the man sounded his horn—that was the last straw, and I shied right off into the big ditch. By the time I had scrambled out, the lorry was far away. Young Jem thought nothing of it, but I had had a very bad

38

fright, and it was long before I got over it.

Young Jem told his father, and he was vexed about it, and told the boy that he had been in too great a hurry. He gave orders that I was to be taken each day on the roads, and the place was to be carefully selected, so that big things could not pass me too close, until I had got used to everything. I got more confidence each day under this method, and gradually lost my nervousness.

CHAPTER VIII

We Go Back to Wootten—School-days are over—Our New Saddles—Tinker's Pretty Ways—And My Wild Ones—Patience and Michael Ride Us for the First Time—We Go Exploring—Little Jack makes Friends with Us—He builds his Indian House—Tinker and I Become Red Indian War-Horses.

AT last the day came for our return to Wootten. That was a very happy day. We had been with Old Jem two months, and we had learnt such a lot. We thought we knew nearly as much as the hunters; they could not condescend to us any more.

We went back in the same order as we had come. Old Jem led me, and his son led Tinker; but now I was wearing a brand-new bridle of well-polished leather with a shining snaffle mouthpiece; and on my back I carried a beautiful new felt saddle, fitting to perfection. And Tinker had just the same. The Colonel had sent the saddles down to be fitted on, so that everything should be right for the children.

Patience and Michael and the Colonel were at the gate to meet us. How excited they were! Patience could hardly speak; she threw her arms around our necks and hugged us.

"Aren't they darlings!" she said.

Colonel Coke was anxious to hear all that Old Jem could tell him.

"The bay pony," he said, pointing at Tinker, "is a perfect pony for the little boy; he has just the right temperament—not too keen—and as lovely a mouth as ever I felt. I have never had to do with a pony more likely to suit a child. I can't speak quite so well of the brown—not for the little lady, I mean—I wish she had had a little more experience, and then I should feel more confident. He hasn't a spark of vice, but he is a little nervous and high-strung, and no breaking will alter that."

He then told the Colonel about that unfortunate ditch, and went on:

"Of course, he is the pick of the two as far as looks go. He would get a prize easy at our Show; jumps like a stag, and much the fastest of the two; but I likes them very very quiet for the little ones. I wouldn't like to see the young lady hurted. I'm not saying he won't come right," he finished, "but he wants watching."

The children mounted then, and rode round the big field. How happy

40

they were, trotting and cantering along together, and how I loved carrying Patience!—she was a feather-weight after Young Jem.

"Much Old Jem knows," I thought; "I wouldn't hurt a hair of her darling head."

"I had the cruppers fitted," said Old Jem as he left. "Always cruppers for grass-fed ponies. Comfort first and fashion afterwards."

Every day now we went out for a ride. Patience and Michael would come to our field and call us; they always had something nice for us, so we trotted up at once. They slipped on our halters and led us up to the stable, tied us up to the manger, and gave us each a tiny feed while they put on our saddles and bridles. Murphy had taught them how to do this on the old pony, and Patience was very good at it, though Michael sometimes needed a bit of help. Often we went round the farm with the Colonel on his hunter, Moonlight, and sometimes we all three went off further; and there were some lovely lanes and moorland quite near, where we never met any of those horrid motors.

The children got on with their riding. Every day they seemed more down in their saddles, and firmer in their seats; and every day they enjoyed their rides more. They had both ridden quite a lot on the old pony, and he had taught them their ABC; but he was so stiff and old that he could hardly go out of a trot, and of course the children were longing to canter and gallop, and as that was just what Tinker and I wanted too, we all enjoyed ourselves very much.

We liked going to so many different places, and we wanted to explore, just as much as they did.

When spring came round again and it was warmer, they often took their lunch with them, and then we could go further; and when summer came again there were very few places within ten miles that we had not been to.

Just about this time, too, we made real friends with Jackie. He was eight years old now, three years younger than Michael, and a serious little boy rather like Patience, only with brown eyes. He had always seemed a little nervous of us up till now, and never cared much to come into our field. He had a wonderful house built by himself, just outside the fence, and we often watched him there. He had built it of willow branches, woven at the top and tied with willow twigs, and the inside was lined with moss, and very snug it looked. He would spend hours there when the elder children were busy, talking to himself and cooking and doing all sorts of funny things. We understood that he was a Red Indian.

One day Jackie hung over our gate looking at us for a long time. The others had gone off in the motor, and he was all alone. At last he climbed down, opened the gate slowly, and came in. He was a dear little fellow, and we were really very fond of him; he always talked to us so gently and kindly, but he had never ventured in quite alone to visit us before.

He came up to me and stroked my nose and gave me a lump of sugar.

"Would you like to be a Red Indian War-Horse?" he said. He got a long bit of string out of his pocket and tied it to my halter, and led me out of the field. Of course Tinker followed too, so that Jackie had two Red Indian War-Horses.

He tied me up outside his wigwam, and brought me lots of nice things to eat, carrots and hay, and apples and mangolds, so that Tinker and I were quite happy, and there we stayed the whole afternoon. The Colonel was quite pleased when he found us all there later on.

"He will be a horseman one of these days," he said, "if only we can find him the right pony." After that Jackie often came to fetch one or the other of us. He had quite lost all his nervousness.

CHAPTER IX

We are Entered for the Horse Show—Colonel Coke doubts my Behaviour—But I Win First Prize—"The Prettiest Pony in the District"—Tinker Bell gets Third Prize—I Grow Conceited.

IT was now September and the local Show was to be held that week. We were both entered for it, and the children were to ride.

"There won't be many ponies," said the Colonel, "and you should have a good chance; specially Mousie, he is sure the catch the judge's eye. Don't either of you be down-hearted if you don't win a prize. There is no system of judging yet that provides for the judge being sure of picking out the best child's pony. All he can say is that, as far as he has seen, the pony is quiet and well-mannered and well-shaped, but many a time the best child's pony gets passed over."

I saw him glance at Tinker, and wondered if he was remembering what Old Jem had said about me. I felt confident, however, that my conduct would be perfection. More than once the Colonel had said to Patience:

"You cannot ride that pony too carefully. He is of an excitable nature, and once he gets really above himself, you will have serious trouble with him. Keep him going steady, give him plenty of work, and never let him get out of control."

Anyway, I had hopes of that prize, and sure enough when the great day came I was picked out—first prize and the red rosette.

Well, that was a glorious moment! and Tinker had a third—not so bad for him. How we galloped round the ring, manes and tails flying, Patience in her new brown coat and breeches, and Michael in his tweed coat and corduroys! "The prettiest pony in the district," I heard the farmers say as I drew up opposite the grand-stand, and I thought so too!

Patience was so excited she couldn't speak, and when the judge asked her and Michael if they had been out with the hounds yet, their cup of joy was full. They hadn't yet started on their hunting career, but it was lovely to feel that the judge thought they were regular followers.

43

That was a great day! My head was full of dreams! What a pony I was! First prize! How I should show them the way in the hunting field!

Patience and I would always be in front! What obstacles we should jump! Brooks, gates, would be nothing to us! My head spun round with dreams.

Mrs. Coke came up with a friend to look at us.

"What a charming couple of ponies!" said the lady; "and how much better they look with their manes and tails on! What distinguished little heads, and legs like deer! I like these moorland ponies ever so much better for children than those hunter-bred ones, and they are safer, too, riding about in rough country, but they are so hard to get."

"Yes," said Mrs. Coke. "There are plenty of them on the moors, but people don't often take the trouble to get them young enough to make them quiet, and to break them properly; but they are well worth the extra trouble, we think."

"I suppose you wouldn't sell the brown?" said the lady.

"No," said Mrs. Coke. "Patience loves him, and I am sure she wouldn't part with him for anything in the world. We couldn't sell either of them; but really we think Michael's pony, the bay, is the better of the two; he has a quieter temperament, and that is everything for a child."

She patted Tinker kindly.

I tossed my head and snorted. Didn't they trust me yet? What did they think I was going to do? Nothing would have induced me to hurt Patience, and they ought to have understood that by this time.

Of course Tinker had never been quite the pony I was, not so good-looking, and not so fast; really he had done pretty well, and he ought to have been well satisfied with his third prize.

How we showed off as we started homewards, heads high and stepping daintily! Everyone turned to look at us. How proud we were of ourselves and our rosettes! And Patience and Michael were riding so well. There was not a child there whose heart did not warm towards us. "If only I could have a pony like one of those," they must have thought.

my head are full of dreams; where a bird I went

When we got home everyone came to our field and gave us something. I had never had so many oats in my life.

I don't know whether it was this, or whether I was too puffed up altogether, but the very next day a dreadful thing happened.

CHAPTER X

The Tragedy of My Life—I Refuse to Pull Up—Patience is Thrown—I Rush to Wootten for Help—Patience is Injured—I am Broken-Hearted—Jack Tries to Comfort Me—I am Sentenced to be Sent Away—Patience and I are sorry together—"No One wants an Excitable Pony"—But at last the Butcher Buys Me.

I KNOW we were both feeling very fresh that morning after the Show, because when the children came to fetch us we gave what they called a mane-and-tail display, and we only did that when we were feeling extra cheerful. Usually we walked up to them slowly to receive our oats, and they slipped the halters gently over our ears. Sometimes, if we happened to be lying down, we would let them halter us as we lay, pretending we were still half-asleep. We would then get up with a tremendous heave and each give a great stretch, first one hind leg and then the other, with our noses pulled right into our chests; this always made the children laugh. But on the mornings when we felt extra fresh, we would start galloping directly they came to fetch us. We would gallop round and round them, going so fast that Patience used to say she could see nothing but flying manes and tails. When we had done this some half-dozen times we gave each other a signal and dashed straight up to them, pulling up suddenly at the very last moment with wild-looking eyes and manes and tails flying.

They quite understood it was all a joke, and they loved it; and then we would drop our heads, looking as mild as milk, and allow them to halter us.

On this particular morning, we had such a tremendous gallop that it was quite clear that we were very fresh, and when we eventually drew up right in front of the children, Tinker made three loud defiant snorts through his nose, pretending to be a wild horse. A great many boys would have been scared, but Michael liked it. They led us into the stable then and saddled us, and we all went out together for one of our favourite rides.

The whole world was turning russet, brown, and gold, and the going was just perfect, after some steady rain in the night.

Patience was so pleased and proud of my success that she could not make enough fuss of me, and I was a very proud pony and doing my best to keep up my reputation. I picked up my feet and trotted as they say a Welsh pony does at Islington. I galloped like a racehorse. Four miles from home the Colonel left us; he had an appointment to keep, and went home a short way. Our way lay along the top of the moor, with two more lovely grass gallops, and then only a quarter of a mile along the road home. The children were practising cracking their whips, and very difficult they found it; they had often watched Jack, the Whipper-in, but it was not quite so easy as it looked. They were longing to get out hunting, but the Colonel was not going to allow this until they could both sit in the right position over a little fence.

We had a glorious gallop, racing neck to neck, Michael practising the racing seat, which he had no business to do, and Patience riding very carefully, doing her best to keep to the rules her father had taught her. The children were always like this. Michael hated rules, and was all for speed. Patience liked to do everything in just the best way possible; she wanted to get on with her riding; nothing was too much trouble, and she was on the right lines to make a first-class rider; but of course she was still inexperienced. We were now nearly home; just one more gallop, and then we would walk soberly down the grass slope and down the last bit of road, so as to come in cool. Whether it was that we had been going a bit too fast, or whether it was too many oats the day before, or being puffed up with my prize, I do not know, but as we started on this last quarter-of-a-mile gallop with its springy, inspiring turf, the thought crossed my mind: "Why stop at the top? Why not gallop down this gentle slope to the road?"

We had reached our usual stopping-place just where the turf led downwards, and Patience was taking a pull at me; but I pushed my head out obstinately, and instead of slowing down I went a little faster, and we tore on faster than ever. Of course I wasn't running away, far from it. I was going to stop at the road and walk quietly home; but the feel of that turf was good—why should we stop before it was necessary?

I had often heard the Colonel say, "Never gallop down hill unless your pony is well in hand," and now I found out exactly what he meant.

48

Patience was a good rider for her age, but she hadn't, at thirteen years old, had much experience; and it does need some skill to stop an excited pony, who has got his head down and means galloping, once you get on a down-hill slope. I found that, without meaning it, I was going faster and faster. I could hardly have stopped if I had wanted to. We were galloping alongside a little wood now—just flying—and Patience, though she took a pull at me now and then, was really just as happy as I was.

There were branches overhanging the grass track, but plenty of room for me to pass under them. I never gave a thought to my rider.

Suddenly there was a sound of crashing boughs. Patience loosened her hold of the saddle, gave a lurch to the left, and fell in a heap.

This terrified me so much that I could not stop to think. I fled down the hill, and down the road. I whisked in at Wootten gate, up the drive and into the stable yard, calling for Murphy at the top of my voice.

He was out in a moment and in the saddle. He knew which way the children were coming, and in five minutes we were back on the moor. The first thing we saw was Michael, who was off his pony and standing just at the place where Patience had fallen. I felt so scared I didn't know what to think. I had never had such an experience before. But things weren't as bad as I feared. Patience was sitting up, looking very white and saying: "It wasn't Mousie's fault; I ought to have taken a pull at him a little sooner."

Michael was as white as a sheet, too; he told Murphy that Patience had lain quite still for ever so long without moving.

Murphy led me home and Patience walked. Tinker and Michael brought up the rear. I was so nervous and upset that I kept shying at all sorts of things. I seemed to see a danger in every bush. All this had happened so suddenly.

I knew I had been wrong, and in the stillness of the night I was able to think over the whole thing.

I never saw Patience the next day, and that worried me. Usually she was out directly after breakfast, whatever the weather was, to see that I was all right and give me a lump of sugar. I heard later that she was to be kept in bed for three days, so as to make sure that no harm had come of her tumble.

Jack came along later, and called me up to the rails and whispered:

"She can't come today, Mousie, she has been concussed."

Later on the Colonel came to look at me, and Murphy too, and they had a long talk together. It was not the accident itself that made them look so grave, and as they talked I began to feel very down-hearted.

"That pony is a bit too much for a beginner," said the Colonel. "Old Jem warned us. He has not got the right temperament; this nervousness and excitability needs a firm hand. We shall have to part with him, Murphy; we cannot risk this sort of thing happening again."

Murphy shook his head sorrowfully. He loved me and was very proud of me, but he was devoted to little Miss Patience, and he said sadly that he knew the Colonel was right. "In another year," he said, "when Mousie is five years old and reaches his full strength, it is not likely that he will be any quieter."

"The children must go on with Tinker for a bit," said the Colonel, "and we shall have to sell the brown. I dare say we may hear of a child who has had a bit more experience; but we can't risk Miss Patience on him again."

It took a long time for me to think all this out. What a fool I had been. Was I not to have a second chance? It really seemed rather hard.

My little mistress was broken-hearted; she used to come into the field and kiss my nose. "It's all my fault," she said; "why aren't I a better rider?" And when she said this it came over me quite clearly what a bad pony I had been.

She was never allowed to ride me again.

"The Colonel's right for sure," said Murphy. "If they do a thing once, and they are ridden under the same circumstances, they will do it again."

So I was left in the field, and Tinker was taken out regularly, one day with Patience, and the next with Michael.

They tried to find a buyer for me, but it was always the same story. Children who could ride an excitable pony like me were scarce, and they have any number to choose from. What everybody seemed to want was a quiet pony like Tinker, and not a first-class excitable pony like me. My opinion of myself went down and down.

The winter went by, and I stayed in the field doing nothing. "In the spring," said the Colonel, "we shall have to sell him, even if he goes to drag a cart."

Another lovely spring came, and it was now May. I was just five years old.

The Colonel gave up the idea of finding a child capable of riding me, and he now decided that I must be idle no longer. A purchaser must be found. Murphy, who knew everybody, would make enquiries, and a fortnight later he had heard of a purchaser—the butcher at Oldbury, the neighbouring town, some twelve miles away.

CHAPTER XI

Parting from Patience—I repent my naughty ways Too Late—Mr. Gammon—My New Home at the Butcher's—I Learn to Draw a Cart—The Slippery Streets and the Hooting Motor-Cars—Charlie takes Me on the Rounds—"Just Look at that Pony"—Happiness and Hard Work.

THE butcher had a good character for looking after his ponies; and being a very fair judge, he jumped at the chance of buying me at a price much below my real value.

"You will have to break him to harness," said the Colonel; "he is a real good pony, but too much for a child."

That afternoon Patience came to bid me good-bye. I was all alone in the stable, and she sobbed as if her heart would break. Why, oh, why had I been so foolish? Surely I could have controlled my high spirits if I had tried a little harder. It was too late now.

Gammon came for me that evening, and I was led away beside another pony. I trotted off cheerfully enough; life was good, and the whole world before me. If I had known more, I should have been more anxious.

Gammon, however, was a good fellow, and I could hardly have fallen into better hands. I found his stable very snug, good straw to lie on, good hay to eat. "No oats for you, young fella, yet awhile," said Gammon. There were three other ponies, and we all became great friends. What a lot they told me; what wonderful lives they seemed to have lived!

Gammon himself broke me in to harness. He was very slow and careful, so that I found things quite easy. Every afternoon he would spend an hour teaching me. First of all I had to get used to the collar; it was, I thought at first, a frightful thing to look at, but he was very gentle, and let me look and smell at everything. In a day or two he took me down the road all harnessed up, so that I felt very proud, and then by degrees I learnt to drag the cart. How difficult it was to turn round between those shafts, and going down hill was worse still! The first time he got me on a down hill, and I had to put my weight into the breeching and hold the cart back, I broke out in a cold sweat with fright. But he was very gentle and careful and we had no set-backs, and at the end of a week I began to do a little work each afternoon. Gammon himself drove me. I was not fit for the young men yet. "They are in too much of a hurry," said Gammon.

Each day I grew in confidence, but there was a great deal to terrify me. How hard it was to keep my legs on those slippery streets! A dozen times a day I was nearly down; it was just like walking on ice, but after a bit I seemed to get a sort of knack of keeping on my legs. Then there were those awful motor-cars.

"What with the slippery streets and the motors, it's not fair on the horses," Gammon used to say.

They went at such a pace, they passed so close, many a time I thought my last hour had come. They seemed as if they let off their horns just on purpose to frighten me. Sometimes they made a terrific bang, and I thought the houses would surely fall upon me; and then the horrible smell, so much worse to us than to human beings. I could never have borne it if I had not had confidence in Gammon, but he was so understanding, and kept me to start with on the quieter roads, I knew he would protect me, and I gradually got bolder. At the end of a week's careful driving I was handed over to Charlie.

"Now, Charlie," said Gammon, "I know I can trust you or I should not let you drive this pony. He is only a five-year-old, he is nervous and excitable, and he has not got the best of characters, but he is a good one. Go very carefully. Only take him the quiet round, and don't give him a single oat until we know he is all right."

Charlie was a good driver, and a real horse-lover, and I made progress each day. Things seemed to get easier, and at the end of the week Charlie said to me:

"Now, Mousie, you have been a good boy, the Boss says you may start oats next week, but not till Tuesday."

Those oats were good. After a hard morning's work, it was a treat to come in and have a drink and then a real good feed. I soon learnt to shout for my oats just like the other ponies, and paw with my fore leg to make Charlie hurry up. First, one feed a day, then two, and then, when I had been going quietly for a month, three feeds.

53

What life they put into me! How I flew down the road! I loved to hear my feet rattle. No whip was needed for me. Charlie prided himself that he never had to touch me. How proud he was of me, and how proud I was of myself!

"Just look at that pony!" I often heard people say admiringly, as I sped down the road—one, two, three, four; one, two, three, four went my feet, as quick as you could count!

"Plenty of work, plenty of food, that's the motto," Charlie would say, as he measured out my oats exactly. The measure was full to the brim, not an oat too many, not an oat too few.

This life just suited me. I wanted hard work and felt the better for it; but I often thought regretfully of my old home, and the green grass, and the shady trees, and the dear friends I had left.

CHAPTER XII

I Make Friends with Firefly—The Story of Her Life—Foolish Mr. R.—The Rough and Careless Grooms—Firefly is Hurt—Smoke and Flames in the Stable—The Brave Little Stable Boy—Saved Just in Time—Firefly's Knees are Broken—So She is Sold to Mr. Gammon.

STANDING in the stable next door to me was a lovely chestnut pony called Firefly. She and I made great friends, and she used to tell me stories of her life.

She was the prettiest little creature—such a fine skin, and her tail carried beautifully, the hair without a kink in it—one of the aristocracy, there was no doubt of it. She didn't much like dragging a cart; she found it heavy, and she often told me how she loved galloping on the green turf. "It's better than a feed of oats to me," she would say.

She was only seven now. She had started life with the most wonderful expectations, but somehow or other everything had gone wrong.

She had been born in a paddock. I think she was quite thorough-bred, and her early years had been most successful. Her owner expected great things from her. She had been broken with the greatest care for a child's riding, and when she was four years old she was carrying off prizes all over the country. She was well known as the best child's pony in three counties.

She was then sold for a big price to a very wealthy man. He wanted her for his little girl. These people, oddly enough, turned out to be friends of Flabber's, and they were something of the same nature.

Mr. R. did not really care about horses. He kept them because it was "the thing" in that neighbourhood. He seldom went into the stable, and everything was left to the head groom.

Mr. R. belonged to the class of the "Rich in Spirit," and his head man was just the same. He had a tremendous opinion of himself. He was always talking about Lords and Marquises and grand places where he had been, and he was always on the look out for tips; the three grooms under him were ill-mannered and discontented like himself. Master and men, they were all "on the make."

Mr. R. paid a very big price for Firefly; he wanted to see his little girl win all the prizes on her. But the child was a shocking bad rider. She rode with short reins, and short stirrups, and was always pulling at her pony; and so poor Firefly could only get along by fighting for her head the whole time. She lost her beautiful manners and got no more prizes, and Mr. R. thought that he had been "done," and often informed his friends that "you could never trust anybody, buying a horse."

Firefly was just as unhappy in the stable as out of it. The grooms were rough and always shouting. They used to shout at the horses as if they were all criminals.

"I ventured to lie down one afternoon," said Firefly, "but I never did it a second time. They shouted and swore at me, and I thought one of them was going to hit me; and then if one stood back in the stall to ease one's fore legs, that was a crime too. We were all to stand up the whole time like a line of soldiers. There was no lack of food—too much of it really; but what we suffered from was lack of exercise. It was seldom I got out for more than an hour a day; and then, when Miss R. rode me, she hurt my mouth so much that I couldn't help pulling, hoping to deaden the pain, and I was thankful to get back to the stables, uncomfortable as they were.

"One day, after I had just come home from a ride, the groom led me so hastily into the stable that I caught my hip, and that is why I am 'down' on one side. The stud groom told his master I had got 'cast' in my stall and had done it then. I could see they didn't like me after this, and were thinking of selling me, and I felt it was unfair.

"Soon after this I had an awful adventure. The grooms used to smoke cigarettes most of the time, and the stud groom would often tell them that trouble would come of it, and 'nobody had ever been allowed to smoke in the stable in his young day.' But as he was always smoking himself, of course he couldn't stop them, and trouble did come. The men had gone off early one evening in November and it was not long before we began to smell smoke. It came from the forage room next door, and steadily got thicker and thicker.

"Then we heard a crackling noise, and soon after we saw bright shoots of flame reflected on the stable wall. It would die down a little and then start again, smouldering and crackling, and each time it got stronger.

"The smoke was suffocating, and we all got terrified. Suddenly the door was flung open, and in came the little stable boy; he hadn't been there long, and we were all fond of him. He was only just fifteen, with a jolly round and freckled face, and he was always kind. He led the horses out one by one and turned them loose in the yard. My turn came last, and I was so terrified that I could hardly bring myself to go with him, but he took off his coat and put it over my eyes, and so led me out. The stable was burnt to the ground before they could get the fire-engine. Nobody ever told Mr. R. what this boy had done. He was too loyal to his fellow-servants to say anything; and the head man let them think it was himself who saved us.

"It was soon after this that one of the grooms took me out exercising. He was very heavy for me, and he put the saddle on so that it was right forward on my shoulders instead of on my back. He went a long way to see some friends, and was late coming home, and he was trotting me fast down hill to make up for lost time when I trod on a loose stone and stumbled. I should have been able to recover myself if the weight had not been all in front, but I couldn't help it, and down I went.

"My knees were broken, but not very badly, and they sold me to Gammon. He is a good master, and I like being with him and Charlie; but I miss galloping on the grass," she ended sadly.

CHAPTER XIII

Dawn's Story—Her Happy Foal Days—The Gardener Who did not Like Ponies—Dawn gets a Bad Reputation—She Refuses to be Caught—Mr. X. Proves that She is not so Bad after All—Miss Bridget falls in Love with Her—But She has to Return to Her Own Little Mistresses—One Can Have Too Much of Petting—Dawn Does a Wicked Thing—Her Character is Gone Again—She too is Sold to Mr. Gammon the Butcher.

THERE was another pony who told me something which I thought very interesting. This pony was Dawn. She was only with us a week. She too was a very pretty, well-bred pony, light grey with black points, and lovely great black eyes. She hardly spoke at all for the first few days, but one day something happened which seemed to unseal her lips, and her story came flowing out. I could see she had been bottling things up and was labouring under a sense of resentment.

This is what happened. One afternoon when we had finished our dinner, and were just going to settle down for our afternoon nap, the stable door opened and Charlie brought in a gentleman to have a look at us.

There were five of us in the stable just then, and we were all in tip-top condition; and Charlie and the boy kept us so well, that we were worth looking at. You don't often see five good-looking ponies together, all under fourteen hands, and the gentleman was very pleased with what he saw. He complimented Charlie, and wanted to know about each one of us.

He laughed when he came to me and saw our stable cat, Tom, curled up snugly on my back. Tom kept me warm and I kept Tom warm, and we were great pals. Tom got down when Charlie talked to him, and went up and rubbed himself against the strange gentleman's legs, sticking his tail right up and purring.

"I am fond of all animals," said the gentleman to Charlie, "but I don't somehow take much to cats. I was reading the other day a book which said: 'Cats do not caress us, they caress themselves upon us.' Do you think the man who wrote that was right?"

"I dunno," said Charlie; "I'm very fond of a good cat myself."

58

In the New Forest.

They went out then, and directly the stable door was shut, Dawn began to speak in an excited undertone. We pricked up our ears. She had been so silent before that she quite surprised us.

"Did you hear what he said about cats?" she said. "That's been my trouble. I'll tell you my whole story. I'll begin at the beginning.

"I had a lovely childhood. I was born in the New Forest—how I wish I was back there now, all among the heather and the old trees. I was sold when I was six months old to a young lady who broke in ponies. She had a lot of us, and her idea was to keep us until three years old and then break us in and get us very quiet for children's ponies.

"We had a very happy time. She understood ponies, and we all wanted to do our best for her. It was indeed easy to do our best, and none of us ever seemed to want to do anything wrong.

"When I was four and a half I was perfectly quiet to ride, and a very pretty pony. Everybody said so. A widow lady bought me for her two little girls. Their ages were twelve and fourteen, and from that moment my troubles began.

"They lived in a new red-brick house in the country, and there was a lovely field for me, but the trouble was that they none of them understood animals at all, nor did the gardener whose job it was to look after me—his name was Giles.

"Giles seemed to take a dislike to me straight off. He was frightened to catch hold of me at the station; he kept on saying, 'Does she kick?' and it was not until the porter had led me some way out of the yard that he ventured to catch hold of the end of the rein. Well, you know how it is, specially when you are young—I was not quite five, and it was my very first place—when people are nervous of us we get nervous of them. It was a bad start, and I felt jumpy from the beginning. And then, when Mrs. Young came out to see me, Giles kept saying: 'Be careful, ma'am! Don't get too near her. I don't like the look of her eye,' and that made me more nervous. Now if she'd come up and given me a lump of sugar, I should have felt quite different, and we should soon have made friends; but this was a bad beginning, and I felt anxious and restless all that night.

"The next morning the eldest girl was to have a ride. Giles came into the field and called. I had been sold as 'easy to catch,' but this wasn't the method I was used to. Giles's call was more of a command than the coaxing and the handful of oats I had been used to, and so, though I went up to him to start with, I felt nervous of him and turned my head away when he put out his hand to halter me. He looked rough, I thought, a bit of a coward, and a bit of a bully—the two always seem to go together. When I turned my head away, of course my hind quarters were near to him, and he made sure I was trying to kick him—and I hadn't even thought of it.

"Well, this happened several times and he began to get cross, and I began to dislike him. He kept commanding me instead of coaxing me, and everyone knows that the only way to catch a pony is by coaxing and tit-bits.

"At last, when I had had enough of it, I walked away and began to graze.

'I don't call that a child's pony,' snarled Giles; 'what's the good of a pony you can't catch?' and he went off and cut a great stick in the hedge.

"The day was hot and the flies trying, and he lost his temper altogether. He came after me with the stick and ordered me to come up and be haltered; but of course I was terrified by that stick, and the more he shouted at me the quicker I made off. He was soon very hot, and the flies were teasing, but they were just as bad for me.

"Half an hour of this and he was in a towering passion, and went off to fetch help from the house. They decided to drive me into a corner and catch me there. By this time I was really nervous—no one had ever pursued me like this before.

"Well, they all came up behind me, and I was soon driven into a corner. I was looking for a way to scramble through the hedge and escape, when Giles sprang at me from behind, thinking to force the halter over my head. I was thoroughly terrified, and naturally I let out—what horse wouldn't? I very nearly caught Giles on the knee, and he was scared to death.

" 'That pony is thoroughly vicious,' he said; 'we can't keep a pony like that for our young ladies. I must tell the mistress.' And they all went away.

"I was left alone for a week. Sometimes they came and looked at me over the gate, but no one ventured in: I was considered dangerous. I was in disgrace.

"At the end of a week Mrs. Young brought a friend of hers to see me, Mr. X.

" 'I am worried to death about this pony,' she said. 'I paid a big price for her, and now it turns out that she is vicious. She is not at all the pony I want for my children, and the seller won't have her back.'

" 'A pretty pony,' Mr. X. said as he came through the gate. He put his hand in his pocket for a lump of sugar, and talked to me softly. Mrs. Young remained safely on the far side of the gate.

" 'I warn you she's vicious,' she said anxiously.

"I ventured up timidly and snuffed his coat; it smelt good, and I took the lump of sugar.

" 'That's funny,' said Mrs. Young. 'She won't let Giles get near her.'

" 'Perhaps your man doesn't quite understand horses,' said Mr. X.

" 'He thinks he does,' said Mrs. Young doubtfully.

" 'I'll tell you what I'll do,' said Mr. X., 'if it would be any help to you. I'll send my groom for her tomorrow and we'll find out what she's really like. My little girl has had plenty of experience, and if she rides her a time or two, we'll soon find out what she's made of.'

"The next morning, the groom came for me. He was a very different person from Giles, and I should soon have let him catch me; but I had been so scared by being chased about, that it wasn't to be done in a minute.

" 'We'd better drive her up slowly into the stable,' said the groom; 'that'll be simplest, but don't let her hurry; we don't want her to go out of a walk, or we'll only make her wilder.'

"Well, they drove me up slowly into the stable and there was a feed waiting for me in the loose-box. Of course I let myself be caught then, and we were soon on our way to Old Orchard.

"When we arrived, Honey, the groom, tied me up and patted me and gentled me all over.

" 'She seems quiet enough, sir,' he said to Mr. X.

" 'Well, turn her out now, and we'll let Miss Bridget ride her tomorrow if she's quiet, but you'll have to take your time over catching her. She seemed shy when I saw her the other day.'

"The next morning Honey came for me; he had his pockets full of oats, and what with those and his soft country voice, I let myself be caught in a very few minutes.

"He soon saw I was quiet enough, and Miss Bridget was delighted with me. She was a great little rider, and thoroughly enjoyed herself as she cantered along by her father's side. 'She's got the loveliest mouth,' she said, 'and she *can* gallop.' How I wished that I had been bought by Mr. X.! I loved little Bridget.

"They kept me for a week, and Bridget rode me each day, and everything went smoothly. Honey got me quite easy to catch again; he only had to call me, when I went straight up to him, and he gave me my oats and slipped the halter over my head.

"Mrs. Young came over to see me; she was delighted. She saw Honey catch me and Bridget riding me, and she seemed to think that perhaps after all I might do for the children. Mrs. Young said that Bridget and I together made the prettiest pair, and she wished that her little girls rode as nicely. Giles came to fetch me next morning.

" 'You won't have any trouble with her,' said Honey. 'Just coax her to follow you into the stable, and she'll be all right.'

" 'I don't like the look of her eye,' said Giles sourly, as he led me off. Honey sighed. 'Give a dog a bad name...' he said half to himself as he turned back to the stable.

"Things were better after that, but Giles never had patience to catch me; he was rough and suspicious and he was nervous. But Mrs. Young insisted on me being driven up slowly to the stable as Mr. X. had advised her, so that things were not nearly so bad as they had been, and went smoothly enough for a time. The children used to ride me in turns; they had had some riding lessons, but they knew nothing about animals at all—they didn't even keep a dog—and that made it difficult. In fact, nobody in the whole household understood animals, though Mrs. Young meant to be very kind. The children meant to be kind too, at least everybody always said how kind they were and how fond of their pony, but sometimes I used to wonder... Anyway, this 'kindness' was in the end my undoing."

Dawn paused and sighed heavily. "I am afraid of telling you the rest," she said. "I know you will be shocked, you are all so good and well-behaved, but what that man said—'Cats do not caress us, they caress themselves upon us'—set me off; but we'd better go to sleep now, it's getting late."

"Oh, do go on," we all called; "we would rather hear about a bad pony than a good pony any day."

Thus encouraged Dawn went on with her story.

"It was this way," she said. "I have never cared from the beginning to be 'messed about'; some ponies love it, some don't mind, and some hate it. Mr. X. understood this well enough. The children brought him to see me one day, and they both started patting me and hugging me and kissing me until I began to get irritable, and I swung round my head pretending to bite, as a warning that I had had enough, and they must be careful or I might give them a nip.

" 'It's quite clear your pony doesn't care for too much petting,' said Mr. X. 'She wants to tell you that one pat is enough, and she doesn't care about any more. Some ponies are like that and if you are wise children you will understand.'

"But they didn't want to understand. The truth is that they patted me to please themselves because I felt warm and silky and alive. I do not call that kindness. How can it be kindness to us if we do not enjoy it? You don't often meet a well-bred pony who does care about it, and I do think that human beings, with all their intelligence, ought to be able to take a hint.

"I think this was one of the reasons why Mr. X. said to their mother one day: 'She is a bit too good a pony for the children at present, what they want is a regular Dobbin.'

"One day it was wet, and I suppose they couldn't go out and were rather bored. Gladys came first and patted me, and I was pleased; but when she went on, patting and stroking and whining, after a bit I got irritable. I swung my head round and pretended to bite several times, but it was no good, she only came back and began again, 'Dear little Dawn, pretty little pony!' until I was almost crazy. At last she went away, and then the other child came in, and exactly the same thing started all over again. 'Dear little Dawn, pretty little pony!' a hundred times over, patting me again and again until I was nearly mad.

"At last I could bear it no longer, and I swung round my head and gave her a good bite on the arm. I knew it was very wrong, but I was irritable that day—Giles was always careless about my digestion—and every little thing seemed to worry me.

"Well, she fled from the stable screaming, and later her mother came, and Giles, and they talked and talked, and I learnt that the doctor had been sent for, and there was a big black bruise. I knew no harm would come of it; my teeth were clean enough, and I was wicked enough to feel some satisfaction at what I had done.

" 'I knew she was a bad-hearted one,' said Giles; 'you've only got to look at her eye.'

"Mrs. Young had always thought I had a beautiful eye, but she decided to sell me, and that is how I am here.

"What I want is justice and not slobber," she ended angrily. "Now you're shocked, I know, and I wish I hadn't told you."

I certainly was a little bit shocked, though I tried not to show it. personally I never minded how much I was petted and kissed, but as I grew older and saw more of the world, I realized that some ponies—and specially the well-bred, nervous ones—are very irritable and easily upset, and dislike being too much petted; and if they feel like that it does seem hard that they should be expected to bear it patiently.

CHAPTER XIV

I Meet Patience Again and She Drives the Butcher's Cart—Charlie says Good-bye—Claud Does Not Understand Horses—I Lose My Confidence and Fall in the Street—I Run Away and Am Brought Home—The Cart is Smashed and I am Covered with Bruises—Mr. Gammon decides to Sell his Ponies—Mr. Greengrocer Becomes My New Owner.

I HAD been with the butcher six months and was now in tip-top condition. Everything went well. Gammon and Charlie were thoroughly pleased with me, and I was very happy. I loved the hard regular work and the good oats.

One morning, when we came back from the round, I saw a well-known figure standing outside the shop.

It was Patience! How glad we were to meet! And her pocket was full of good things for me—sugar, apple, and a carrot.

"Well, Miss," Gammon was saying, "he's the best pony we've got. No day is too long for him, he never does no wrong, enjoys his work, and eats up his dinner. Would you like to go round to the stable with Charlie and see the other ponies while you're waiting for the Colonel?"

This just suited Patience; nowhere was she happier than in a stable, and Charlie led me off with Patience walking beside us.

He told her all about me, and what he said made me feel proud and pleased. The road outside our stable was very quiet, and Charlie asked Patience if she would like to drive me down to the end of it. She jumped at the idea, and in a second she was in the butcher's tiny seat, and I was flying down the road as fast as I could lay legs to the ground. I wanted to show what I could do. She turned me round at the end of the road, well pleased, and walked me back to the stable.

Charlie showed her the other ponies, and then she had to go. She gave me a hug and shook hands with Charlie.

"Oh, Charlie, I do thank you for making him into such a good pony," she said; and she was off down the road running hard for fear she might keep the Colonel waiting.

"That's the sort!" said Charlie to his mate, and often after when he was grooming me, he would say, "Your little Missus *would* be pleased if she saw you now," or, "Your little Missus wouldn't like to hear you had been so impatient waiting this morning!"

I had been with the butcher two years, and very happy ones they were—plenty of work, plenty of oats, and a kind master; but there was a bad time coming. One morning Charlie came into the stable.

"Mousie boy," he said, "I am leaving you. I've got a chance of a better job, and sorry as I am to go, I've got to think of my young lady, or we shall never get married at all."

At the end of the week Charlie had gone, and from that day everything went wrong. The young man Claud, who came to look after me, couldn't compare with Charlie. He had a motor-bike, and he preferred motors to horses. He never took the trouble to feed me properly; sometimes I had half my share of oats, sometimes I had double. Once he forgot to give me my water before my oats, and gave it me after, and what a pain I did have. I rolled on the ground in agony, and the vet. had to be sent for. "Colic," he said; "improper feeding."

Then when we were out, instead of driving at a steady, even pace, with a light feeling on the reins, he would dash along one moment, and pull up the next, so that I never knew where I was.

Worst of all, he would keep tugging at my mouth with the reins. I would far rather he had beaten me. Gammon spoke to him several times, but it was no good. He thought he knew, and he didn't want to learn from anybody.

One day he thought he would race me against another butcher driving a motor, and he picked up the whip and hit me. I went off full gallop, and I think he was frightened, for he soon pulled me up. But all this sort of thing seemed to unnerve me: I never knew where I was, and I was always afraid that I should feel that whip again.

One day we were going down High Street; it was down hill, and the traffic was awful. The road was like glass, and I was feeling nervous of that, and the whip, and the huge, ugly motors. I had no confidence in this young man like I had in Charlie. All of a sudden my legs went from under me, and I was down. Claud was shot out of the cart, and lay insensible, and I lay where I had fallen, paralyzed with terror. Suddenly I heard behind me a great motor-lorry approaching! My old fears returned. I made sure that it was coming straight for me. I leapt to my feet and fled down the street, with everyone shouting and running out of the way. At the bottom there was a sharp turn for home. I knew I should never get round safely at that pace, but I was going too fast to pull up. I saw the danger ahead, but I could do nothing to help myself, and I crashed into a lamp-post. The cart was smashed, and so was the harness, and I was a mass of cuts and bruises.

Somebody led me home, a miserable figure with all the courage gone out of me, and all my pride gone. Gammon was much upset.

"It's not fair," he said; "they have driven us off the roads. It's no longer safe for horses, and the young men aren't fit to look after a horse neither!"

Poor Gammon! Fond as he was of a good horse, he felt that the time had come to take to motors. One of the other ponies had nearly died of a chill, owing to Claud's carelessness; another had slipped down and broken his knees. I was unable to do a stroke of work for a month, and when I was well again I learnt that "the Boss" had made up his mind to sell us all. Just at first I hardly realised how my good fortune was leaving me. But gradually it dawned on me that I was not by any means the pony I used to be, and was not likely to sell well.

"That pony doesn't look up to much," said a friend of Claud's who came to look at us.

"No," said Claud, "he's a nervous, silly little brute, and smashed up his cart a month ago when I was driving him, and nearly killed me, and he's never been the same since."

How I wished I could speak! I would tell them a few home truths. It was all Claud's fault. He fed me so badly, that is why I looked so poor and he had frightened me half out of my wits. The next week we were all to be sold at Oldbury Fair, and I soon learnt by the remarks of people who came in and out that I was not likely to sell at all well. In the first place, I was still looking a miserable object; and then I had run away with the cart for no reason at all, so they said, and my character was lost.

Gammon, who used to be so proud of his ponies, was now so downhearted that he seemed to have lost interest in us.

"They'll make no sort of a price," he said, "with all this craze for

Something led me home

motors, and it's not fair, the roads were made for horses; and now they've been made so that horses can't go on them; and they're still the cheapest for my sort of work, anyhow. And what is a motor, anyway?—nought but a dummy!

In spite of all this discouragement I could not believe it when I was put up for auction and the highest price bid was £8!

Eight pounds! For me!

My purchaser was a greengrocer who lived two streets away. I knew him well by sight. I had often seen his pony, and pitied her; she looked so rough, so dull-eyed, so poor.

"No need to look like that, all the same," I thought. "Of course the cart's heavy, a lot heavier than Butcher's, but I shouldn't look as draggle-tailed as that if I was in the shafts."

However, we live and learn, and I was soon to learn just why poor Queenie had always looked so miserable, and why she had quite un-accountably—in Greengrocer's opinion—died the month before.

CHAPTER XV

A Bad Home—Mr. Greengrocer talks Kindly but acts Cruelly—Mrs. Greengrocer and Her Dog Bob—An Uncomfortable Stable—The Hay is Bad and the Stable Boy steals My Oats—A Miserable Life.

NOW Greengrocer thought that he was a very good man, and most of his neighbours seemed to think so too. He was a flabby, white-faced sort of man, fond of hearing his own voice—he often spoke at meetings—and was one of those superior people who are never wrong.

He would have been horrified if anyone had suggested that he was cruel to animals. He was very fond of them—so he said—and couldn't bear to see them knocked about. This was true. I remember him talking to a boy once who was ill-treating a pony, and of course all he got was a lot of "cheek" back for his pains.

Now though he professed to be so soft-hearted, any animal who got into his hands had a shocking bad time. The truth was he was full of talk, but he had never taken the trouble to find out how animals ought to be treated, and he was so confident that nothing he did could be wrong that he never learnt. We want knowledge and justice before kindness, and that is what a great many soft-hearted people never seem to understand. We think that kindness, without knowledge and justice, is just slobber.

Mrs. Greengrocer was much the same. She was always petting and kissing her big fox terrier Bob, an odious, ill-mannered creature, I thought. He used to come yapping round my heels, and one day he even dared to nip me, but fortunately I succeeded in giving him a sharp kick and sent him home squealing, and he never tried that again.

Bob was always in trouble; if it wasn't one thing it was another. He growled at the postman, he snapped at the baby next door, he chivvied the sheep down the road, he killed old Mrs. Tomkin's favourite cat, and as for quarrelling, he was at the bottom of every fight in our street. How the other dogs did dislike him! But you really could not blame him. Mrs. Greengrocer had never taught him a thing. And he was own brother to Mrs. Gammon's Ship, but how different they were! Ship was

71

a model of deportment.

I heard Mrs. Greengrocer say once to Mrs. Gammon, "However did you manage to stop Ship fighting?"

"I punish him when he does wrong just as I would one of the children," said Mrs. Gammon. "I shouldn't let one of them hit another child, not should I let my dog attack another dog without making sure that he suffered for it. If he won't do what I tell him, I hit him, that's my method."

"Oh, I call that cruel!" said Mrs. Greengrocer. "I couldn't hurt a dumb animal."

But Mrs. Gammon knew that her method was the right one. She knew that animals and children who are allowed to go their own way will be ruined and come to a bad end.

Her Ship, when I first went to live at the butchers, was inclined to be a bit quarrelsome. He was then just over a year old, and he thought he owned the street. Mrs. Gammon used to take him out on a lead, and if he saw another dog coming he would start growling, and stiffen up in a fighting attitude. Mrs. Gammon would scold him and take him home in disgrace, to show him he was wrong, and he would drop his tail and look ashamed. One day, however, an Airedale came along. Ship was very jealous of Airedales; they were so big and strong, and he bristled all over when he saw this one. The Airedale took no notice of him at all, and Mrs. Gammon spoke sharply to him, but it was no good; his temper was too much for him, and he danced on the tips of his toes, his eyes alight with anger, and all the hair on end down his spine. Mrs. Gammon had a little switch with her, and she gave him two sharp strokes and scolded him, and took him home and tied him up in disgrace. A few lessons like this soon cured him, and now he was a really nice-mannered dog who always did what he was told.

Mrs. Greengrocer was quite different. Her Bob was bred just the same way as Ship, and came from the same litter, but you could not meet two dogs more unlike, and it was all because of the different way in which they had been brought up.

When Mrs. Greengrocer took Bob out walking, and he started growling, she got nervous. She would stand still instead of taking him on, and say, "Come Bob! come Bobby! good dog! good doggy! come along! bad dog! bad boy! bad doggy!" and so on. Of course, this sort of thing had no influence with Bob; he would linger, growling and snarling, and as he got stronger he got worse. If he had been alone he would soon have been taught his place by other dogs, and would have learnt manners, but with his mistress to protect him, he always got off somehow or other, though he often said the most insulting things. He got steadily worse. Mrs. Greengrocer never thought of punishing him. She never even scolded him—not to make him mind. She was too full of relief each time that a row was avoided. The insults and bad words he flung at other dogs got worse and worse. He now started fighting. First came a torrent of bad words, and then he would fling himself at a passing dog, and he soon got himself thoroughly disliked.

Every now and then the other dog would go for him, and then there was a regular dust-up. Mrs. Greengrocer was in an agony, and often she brought him home with an ear torn or a pad bitten. Bob thoroughly enjoyed these rows.

Being so undisciplined, he began, too, to get surly and bad-tempered. I was told he often growled at his mistress in the house, and as he was never punished he got worse; and at last, one day when he was under the sofa and feeling rather livery, and she wanted to bathe him, he bit her. Altogether he caused so much trouble and anxiety that nobody really minded when he ran out one day and was killed by a motor. Mrs. Greengrocer cried a good deal, but Mr. Greengrocer had several times said they would have to get rid of him, and in her heart of hearts Mrs. Greengrocer knew that he really had become unbearable.

All this was the result of ignorance. Mr. and Mrs. Greengrocer were kind-hearted enough in a sloppy sort of way, but they did not know how to treat a dog. They did not know either how to treat a pony, and I was soon to learn how seriously this would affect me.

My heart sank the minute I was taken into the stable. I had always been lucky up till now. Most of my time I had lived in the open air, and that is best of all; but when I was indoors I had always had a homely, quiet, airy stable. This stable was quite different. It smelt damp and mouldy; it smelt of petrol and motor-cars. It was a noisy, clattering, draughty place, where one could hardly move without breaking an old wine bottle, or upsetting a tin full of nails. Then there was a hen who would lay her eggs in my manger, and of course I didn't like the smell of hens; and the boy never cleaned my manger out, and that spoilt my appetite. The hay was bad, too; Greengrocer was no judge of hay. This was a cheap lot, and most of it was mouldy.

I was to have one feed of oats a day—two pounds by measure—but, unfortunately, the boy whose duty it was to feed me regularly put half of this in his pockets for his livestock at home, so I only got half my share.

There was a little field where I was turned out after my day's work, and here it was pleasant, with green grass and a big shady elm tree, and a little pond at the far end. If it hadn't been for this little field I should have been even worse off than I was. So long as the grass was good I supplemented my poor rations here, and did fairly well; but when the winter came, the grass lost its feeding value, and I got thinner and thinner. I lost all my pluck and fire. Nobody would have dreamt of calling me an excitable pony any more. When January came it was all I could do to drag the cart. My hours were not long—I seldom did more than a morning's work—and the cart was not too heavy; but all this poor food told on me, and I lost all my strength.

Another thing made life very hard. Greengrocer would not take me regularly each month to the forge to have my shoes seen to. He had an idea that there was no need for attention until the shoes were worn out. He didn't realize that my feet were growing the whole time, and that they needed cutting down at regular intervals. With my shoes needing attention badly, and the slippery roads, it was all I could do to keep my feet, and that made the work just twice as difficult.

CHAPTER XVI

A Kind Lady Gives me some Sugar—Winter Comes—The Pond is Frozen—Nobody Gives me any Water and I am Dying of Thirst—Mr. Gammon to the Rescue—My Life is Saved—But I Feel the effects of Ill-Health—I Become a Miserable Drudge.

A LADY came up one day, when I was waiting in the street. She gave me a lump of sugar, and I felt that she knew how hard life was for me, and that she was very sorry for me. She noticed my ill-fitting harness and my wretched condition, and she would have liked to help me, but she did not see how to do it.

She peeped into my mouth.

"Why, he's only seven, poor little chap! I thought he was sixteen at least," she said to the child with her. Greengrocer came back then, and they talked a little about me. "A well-shaped pony," she said. "Is he an Exmoor?"

"I think he is," said Greengrocer; "he's a good pony enough, but he's got a good home. I'm quite silly about my animals."

"Ah!" said the lady, "he's looking a bit poor."

"That's the breed, ma'am; mustn't overfeed these ponies. But he's twice the pony he was when I bought him; he has the best of everything."

"I've got one at home," she said, "and he's round as an apple."

"I dare say," said Greengrocer rather sniffily, and he drove on.

How I did wish that Greengrocer *knew* a little more. He was not a bad-hearted man, and would have been really distressed if I could have told him that I was being slowly starved to death. But things were to get worse still.

Early in February we had a sharp frost. Now I was in the habit, after my work, of spending the afternoon in the field and coming into the stable before dark, when I had my small supply of oats. I had my long winter coat on, and this arrangement was a pleasant one to me.

I used to drink at the little pond each afternoon, and the boy was supposed to water me before I went out in the morning, but he never did. This sharp frost having set in, my pond was frozen. I walked round

75

hoping to find a weak spot which I could break, but it was no good. That evening I was so dry I could not eat my oats or hay, and in the morning I set out to do my work on an empty stomach. Greengrocer didn't seem to notice anything wrong. The frost held, and in the afternoon I could get no water again—nor could I eat my scanty meal.

The next day Greengrocer began to worry. "There's something wrong with the pony," he said to his wife at midday. "I could hardly get him to trot. I shall get that chap Gammon to come and have a look at him this afternoon."

In the afternoon Gammon came. I was glad to see his jolly face; he had always been the best of masters to me, and he thoroughly understood stock.

"There is something wrong," he said to Greengrocer. "He's only half the size he ought to be, and if it wasn't for that long coat you'd see all his ribs; and look at his quarters—why, they ought to be round as an apple, instead of which they're flat as a board. Let's have a look at the hay."

"Poor stuff," he said, sniffing it; "the pony can't live on that, and what's more it will spoil his wind if he eats much of it. What about the oats?" The oats passed inspection, but I longed to tell him that all I saw of them was less than one pound a day instead of two. I think the butcher had his suspicions, because he asked next: "Can you trust that boy of yours? Pack of young rascals I find them! Need watching the whole time. There's an old saying with a lot of sense in it: 'There's nothing like the Master's eye to make the horse grow fat.' What about water?" he asked next.

"Oh, the boy gives him a drink each morning," said Greengrocer; "and then, of course, there's the pond!"

"Well, that's frozen now," said Gammon. "Let's try him with a drink and make sure he's not thirsty." But the pail was nowhere to be found! The boy had taken it away months ago, to use for feeding the pigs. Greengrocer was getting uncomfortable. He went to the house and filled a bucket. I drank the lot and wanted more; it had only come just in time. "That boy needs watching," said Gammon. "I've got a bit of good hay up at my place, I'll send you round some to go on with. I should feed the

76

No one could say I was conceited now

pony myself if I were you, and you'll find in a week or two he'll pick up."

Well, Greengrocer took more care after that, and a good thing too. In another day or two I should have got down and never got up again.

The boy was well scolded, and things got a little better. The pail was brought back, but it wasn't often used. Greengrocer was a bad judge of hay, and the boy's rabbits wanted so many oats that I never really got my share.

Greengrocer never learnt how a pony ought to look, if he is well. The real horse-lover knows at a glance. He seemed quite satisfied as long as I managed to drag my cart wearily round the little town; he did not seem to consider what a different animal I should be if only I had decent care, and how proudly I should do my work. There was no pride in me now. "A conceited pony!" that was what Tinker had called me once. No one could say I was conceited now. I had just the dull feeling that I must keep on with the dreary round, and go on and on until the day came when I dropped.

I dare say I should have existed like this for many years; my constitution was excellent, and I was a very hard sort; but it was just existence, not life, and it mattered nothing to me whether I lived or died. There was no pleasure in life. I was too weak and tired to enjoy myself.

And then, when the whole world looked as dark and dismal as it could possibly be, a wonderful thing happened.

CHAPTER XVII

At the End of My Tether—I See Tinker Bell—Patience Once More—"My Darling Mousie!"—Patience and Her Five Pounds—Will She Buy me?—Days of Anxiety—Patience Comes Again—I am Her Pony Once More—She Takes me Back to Wootten—I am a Sorry Sight—Wootten Is Like Paradise—Jack Has Had No Luck with His Ponies—Patience Sets Herself to Bring me Back to Condition as a Mount for Jack—Murphy thinks It May be Possible—The Pride of Tinker Bell.

I WAS dragging my cart wearily along one bright March day, when my master pulled me up near the village post-office. He had lately increased his round—not a good thing for me—and I had not to my knowledge been in this particular village before, and yet as I stood there waiting for him there seemed something familiar about it.

I heard the sound of horses approaching. I raised my head, and I saw coming towards me two ponies, with a girl and boy riding them. The girl was a wiry well-made child of fifteen or so, mounted on a well-bred fourteen-hand pony; and the boy, two years younger, was on a bay pony which looked like an Exmoor. I was too tired to give them more than a glance, and then my head drooped again.

The ponies were pulled up just ahead of me, and the girl's voice, which somehow seemed familiar, said: "Here, Michael, you hold the reins, while I go into the post-office, and then we must go straight home, or we shall be late."

My weary brain was trying weakly to think why that voice was so familiar, when suddenly a loud whinny in front of me made me throw up my head. There was the little Exmoor—no doubt of his being an Exmoor now—with his head flung high with that peculiar upward look which only Exmoors have, roaring a welcome at me.

I gazed at him for a moment, and then I realized—there was no doubt of it—it was Tinker Bell.

In spite of the boy's efforts to restrain him he advanced towards me, stretching his soft muzzle out to mine, and breathing words of love and affection. How good it was to meet him again! I had met many ponies since we parted, but never one who had so warm a place in my heart as

Tinker Bell.

At that moment Patience, for of course it was she, came out of the post-office.

"I don't know what's happened to Tinker," called Michael, "but he will talk to that poor miserable little pony."

Patience looked at me hard, and then came up to me. I put my muzzle in her hand, and then raised my head and laid it on her shoulder, knuckering softly into her ear.

"My Mousie!" she said. "My darling Mousie!" And she put her arms round my neck, all travel-stained and filthy as I was, and hugged me. "Michael, don't you recognize him? It's darling Mousie back again."

My heart warmed with loving memories. The happy past came back to me. How good the world was then! How gently warm the sun had shone in those far-off days! How green the grass was! How kind and understanding Patience had always been!

I learnt later that she had asked Murphy to find out who had bought me from Gammon; but Murphy, afraid of letting her know that I had a poor home, had pretended that I had been sold to someone far away, and was quite happy, so that she had made no more enquiries.

At that moment my master came back. Patience was seeking in her pocket for oats, and the well-remembered rustle brought happy days vividly to me.

"Please, Mr. Greengrocer," she said, "can you tell me where you bought this pony, because he is so like a pony that belonged to me three years ago?" The greengrocer told her that he bought me from a butcher at Oldbury Fair. He added:

"I would like to sell him now; he's not strong enough for my work. I want something bigger."

I felt Patience's hand tremble on my neck as she asked:

"How much would you ask for him?"

"Seven pounds," he answered.

"I've got £5 in my bank," said Patience. "Will you promise not to sell him for three days, while I find out whether I can somehow get the rest?"

The greengrocer agreed to this; he evidently did not feel there would be great competition to purchase me.

"Michael, can you remember the address?" she said. They both read it carefully on the side of the cart, and then they rode off. My heart sank as they disappeared, it was as if a cloud had passed across the sun. Could it be possible that I should ever go home again? That would be too good to be true.

Two days passed, two weary days of anxiety, and then, just as we were returning from our morning's round, we saw a small motor pulling up at the door. Out of it stepped the Colonel and Patience.

My heart seemed to stop beating. Patience ran up to me. This time her pockets were bulging—oats, and lumps of sugar, a carrot, and an apple.

"You're right, child," said her father; "it's Mousie, sure enough; he's unmistakable, but he's not worth £7.

My heart sank again, but after a short talk with the greengrocer, who already had a stronger pony in his mind's eye, a bargain was struck, and I was sold for £6.

"May I have him today, please?" asked Patience.

"Certainly, Miss," said the greengrocer, well pleased to be rid of me. "I can take the other pony for my afternoon round; but how are you going to take him?"

"I think," said Patience, "I shall come this evening on my pony and lead him home. Would you be so kind as to give him this feed of oats, because it is a long journey after his day's work?"

The greengrocer smiled; he was by no means a bad-hearted man, and Patience amused him. I was led off to the stable and unharnessed, and the delicious feed put in front of me.

And then I had an anxious time of waiting. Would Patience really come back for me? Would something occur to stop her? Many reasons why she should not come passed through my mind. That smart chestnut pony might jib, or run away, or buck her off, or fall down. Anything might happen. How slowly the time passed! But at last, at 5 o'clock, I heard the sound of ponies' feet. Patience and Michael had come to fetch me. A snaffle was put in my mouth, and Patience, riding Topper, the well-bred young chestnut pony she had been on the day before, led me along gently, walking and trotting, while Tinker Bell snorted triumphantly in the rear. It was a good ten miles, but my heart was light, and though my legs were weary enough, that lightened the journey. Colonel Coke was there to greet us.

"Well, my dear," he said "I am delighted to see the pony back again; and though I do not think you have made a good bargain, so far as money goes, I think you have done quite right. I fear he will never be fit for much, but perhaps after we have fed him up a bit we might be able to get him a good home mowing a lawn or something of the sort."

Patience took me into the stable, and there gave me another delicious feed.

"Not too much, pony," she said as she carefully measured out a small feed, "or you will get indigestion; and be sure to eat your chaff up too."

When I had finished she led me out to the meadow. How well I remembered it! There I found Tinker Bell and Topper. How happy they looked, and how different from me! I was tired and sad, with a ragged mane, and a shabby, half-grown tail. My coat was dirty and coming out in patches. All my ribs were showing, and my quarters drooping and flat as a board. My head was sunk so low between my shoulders that I had difficulty in raising it even for a second or two. And Tinker with his sleek coat, rounded quarters, flying mane and tail, and shining eyes, was exactly the same age as I!

But how wonderful it was to be back home again! It had always been "home" to me. I had nothing to do but eat and wander about and talk to the other ponies. I felt so different from them, however, that it was difficult to talk much. I had no heart for talk, and we did not seem to have much in common, but they were very kind to me. What a sad thing life was! Here was I worn out at seven years old, and I might have been happy and useful for twenty-five years or more.

April was now here, and the grass improving every day. Added to this we each had a feed brought out every evening, which we ate in wooden boxes on the ground. By the end of the month I realized that I was putting on flesh, and, what was better still, I was feeling a little happier in myself.

Then came May, when our world was like Paradise, and I changed my dirty shaggy winter coat for a far smarter sleek and shiny summer one. I began to feel and look more like the others, and we had long delightful talks under the big chestnut tree. It was then that Tinker Bell told me his adventures since we had parted. "Very uneventful," he said, "compared with your life," but to me it seemed he had had a most wonderful career of continuous success and triumph. Not only had he won prizes at Shows for the best child's pony, but he had won prizes at the local Gymkhana for musical chairs, bending race, handy hunter competitions, and no end of things I had never even heard of. He was considered the best pony in the neighbourhood, and Michael the best rider of his age.

This led me on to ask about Jack, who was now eleven; he had been only a little fellow when I left; how was he getting on with his riding?

"Oh, Jack has been unfortunate," said Tinker. "The first pony they got him was very old and slow, and he couldn't make him go. He used to say he thought riding was a very dull affair. Then they changed him for another; he was called Magpie. He had a mouth like iron, and he had been thoroughly spoiled. When he started trotting or galloping, he used to get his head down, and Jack couldn't pull him up, and after a bit he got nervous, and said he didn't like riding. So they sold Magpie, and a good thing too, he was only fit to drag a cart. And last Christmas, when they asked Jack if he would like a pony, he said, 'No, I don't think so.' The Colonel is disappointed about it. He says everyone ought to ride who has a chance, it is the finest education in the world; and his mother is worried too; she says Jack is delicate, but that he'd be right enough if only he'd take to horses. He'd ride all right if he had the right pony. He rides me all right, but I'm too busy."

Tinker gave a self-satisfied snort here, and then he was struck suddenly by a new idea. "Why don't you apply for the job?" he said.

"I should jump at it if I had the chance," I answered rather sadly.

"Oh, you've got a chance!" said Tinker cheerfully.

He told me then that last year Murphy, the Irish groom of whom we were all so fond, had left. The Colonel and his wife had decided to give up their hunters for a bit, and they were out at grass a few miles off. They could not afford them with the children costing so much at school.

They kept the ponies because the children had promised to look after them entirely themselves, and they cost so little out at grass.

"Of course we missed Murphy dreadfully," said Tinker; "but Patience is wonderful; she learnt everything she could from him the last year he was here, and when he was breaking in the Colonel's young horse she used to go out each day on Topper and learn what he could teach her about giving a horse good manners and a good mouth.

"Topper has improved considerably since she started improving him," he added, raising his voice slightly so as to make sure that Topper, who was dozing, should hear. "A horse, and specially a pony, is worth very little without a good mouth and good manners. Murphy said it more than doubled their value."

This conversation gave me a great deal to think about.

Was it too late or was it still possible to make a success of my life?

As to this business of mouth and manners, I could remember well my breaker saying: "This pony has a beautiful mouth and the best of manners." But that was a very long time ago; now I was changed: my mouth felt dead, my body stiff and slow to move; there was no suppleness in me, and as to manners, I had almost forgotten what they meant. It all seemed pretty hopeless; but all the same the idea came back to me very often, and I knew it was in Tinker's mind too. He often talked about "mouth and manners." It was a subject on which he thought he knew a great deal. "You should just see me at a Show," he said.

CHAPTER XVIII

I Make Some Improvement—Murphy is Hopeful—My Lessons Begin—I Turn Out to be a Good Pupil.

AT the end of May Patience brought her father to look at me.

"I want you," she said, "to have a really good look at him. Do you think that if I tried very hard to train him, and teach him all the things which Murphy taught your four-year-old last year, that I might get him right for Jackie?"

"Well," said Colonel Coke, "it may be possible; it is worth trying. He has improved in condition in an unbelievable manner, and of course he was always a beautiful shape. You try and see what you can do. Murphy is coming over to see us tomorrow evening; he knows more about breaking than I do; have a good talk with him."

This was good news. Murphy had always been a friend to me, and what he did not know about horses was not worth knowing. To start with, he was an Irishman, and Irishmen have an instinctive knowledge of horses; then he had been an Army rough-rider, and he knew how to train a young horse. But my heart sank again—I was young no longer. What could training do for a pony who felt so old and so stiff, whose mouth seemed dead, and who could only carry himself as if life was one perpetual down hill?

I awaited Murphy's verdict with deep anxiety.

After tea I watched for them, with my head hanging over the gate, and before long I saw them coming.

"Well, Miss Patience," Murphy was saying as they came into the field, "he used to be a beautiful pony; his only fault was that he was a bit too good for a little girl as you were then; he was a bit too much for you. If it was possible to get him right for Master Jackie it would be well worth while."

"Well, pony," he said softly as he patted me and rubbed my nose "it is a good job you have come back, and you don't look quite as bad as I feared either."

"He has picked up wonderfully in the two months he has been here," said Patience. "He's beginning to look a little bit like his old self. After all, Murphy, he's only just seven now, though he looks so old, and that's in his favour. What do you really think about him?"

"Well," said Murphy, slowly, "I think you may be able to make a good pony of him yet. He has lost all his nervousness and excitability—that was his great trouble when you rode him—but you are sure to find his mouth has been calloused. Ignorant people always jerk the reins to make a pony in a cart go on, and that will, of course, have deadened his mouth. But he used to be such a sensitive little fellow, and so keen to do his best, that I think with careful handling you may be able to re-educate him. Then, of course, over-driving has made him heavy in front, and you will have to try and get him back on his hocks so that he can hold his head high again. You have got plenty of patience, and you have got the knowledge, and if you are willing to spend the time, I think you could do a lot for him. But you must not be disappointed if nothing comes of it. Whether he will ever be fit for Master Jack, I can't say, but it is worth while to try."

"That's good news," said Patience. "I'd do anything to make a good pony of him so that we could keep him. When shall I begin, Murphy?"

"I think he's strong enough to start his lessons now," said Murphy. "I should give him twenty minutes at most each day, that would be quite enough. Start with the exercises dismounted; teach him first the exercise for obeying the leg, and then how to back. You remember how hard we worked last autumn when I was breaking the young horse, and how much the exercises improved your pony. When he is quite sensitive on foot, do the same thing mounted, and then bend him in and out of the trees, so as to get him handy turning. Don't take him out of a walk; you want to get a new set of ideas into his head, and re-educate him, and teach him to carry himself as he used to."

"When will you come back, Murphy," said Patience, her face beaming, "to see how we are getting on?"

"I shall be back in three weeks," said Murphy. "We're very busy just now with the young horses, or I should like to look in before."

Next day my lessons began.

After tea, Patience came to bridle me. She put on me the little snaffle bridle, the very one, I believe, with the bright buckles and pretty headband which I used to wear, and she led me away to the next field, which was quiet and empty. I walked after her stiffly. Though I was feeling pretty well in myself now, I felt I had lost for ever my former spring and energy, and I didn't think I should ever be any different. Instead of dancing along with my head high and my hocks under me, as Tinker Bell and Topper did, I just dragged along, my head low, on a level with my withers, and my legs stiff as pokers.

"Your cart was too heavy, Mousie," said Patience. "But you must cheer up. We shall hope to change all that, and before long you will move again like you used to."

She put her hand in her pocket and produced a handful of oats to encourage me.

"First of all," she said, "I shall re-educate your sides and get them sensitive again, so that you are able to answer to my legs. That will help you to get your hind legs under you, and your head up." She pressed my near side with her crop and pulled the left rein gently, so that I had no alternative but to move my quarters away from the whip. Each time I did right, she gave me a few oats, and that seemed to clear my brain wonderfully and to make things easier. At first my sides felt so dull and dead, I found it very hard to move; but gradually, what with practice and the oats, I got quicker and my sides got more feeling in them. Of course I had learnt it long ago at the breakers, and little by little it came back to me. As my sides began to feel more sensitive, so I began to use my hind legs better, and my head seemed to go up an inch or two.

A few days later Patience began to practise me in "backing," so that I learnt to back at the least touch of the reins. When I was perfect on foot, she got on me, and we repeated the same thing mounted.

Gradually I began to lose that stiff feeling as if a poker went straight from the root of my tail to my ears, and when we began the bending exercises in and out and round about the trees, I began to feel my former suppleness coming back.

"Murphy's coming tomorrow," said Patience one evening. "You will have to do your very best. I do hope he will think you are getting on."

"He's looking brighter, anyhow," said Murphy, when he saw me.

"Let's see how he moves."

Patience got on me, and we did our best. She made me turn on my forehand, she made me walk a figure-of-eight, and she made me back.

"Well done!" said Murphy. "That's splendid! I am sure you will make a good job of him now, Miss Patience! He's quite a different pony. With horses it is the first steps that are the most important, and the hardest to teach. You have got his head well up, and his sides sensitive, and he bends his neck to you. I don't think you will have any more trouble. You want to get him trotting slowly now, head well up, hind legs under him, then stop and back two steps, and then on again. When he is quite supple, try the same thing cantering, but be sure to go very slowly. He needs time to think about things, and to grow new muscles, and get his condition back. And give him plenty of bending exercises at a trot, and I don't think it will be long before Master Jack's hunter is ready for him."

All through the next month we went out for an hour or two hours a day, walking, trotting, and cantering. Gradually, what with good food, and the summer weather, and all these suppling exercises, I felt myself growing younger and my work easier, so that Patience and I seemed to move together as if we had but one mind between us. I could bend through the trees without bumping her knee. I could stop even from a canter and back two steps or more, just as I was asked. I could come up to a gate just as she wanted and open it, and, what is more difficult, come back to shut it again.

I felt years younger. I felt a new pony.

CHAPTER XIX

Jack Has his First Ride—I Take Great Care of Him—Patience Does a Good Bit of Work—We are All Going Back to Exmoor—Michael Comes Home—Preparations for the Journey.

"NOW, Mousie," said Patience one morning, "Jack is going to ride you today, and I want you to be extra good. It is most important."

"Good-morning, Mousie," said Jack, "I hope you are going to like me." He looked at me doubtfully; he did not feel sure whether, after all, he would not prefer to stay at home and look after his rabbits. I stood very still for him to mount, and then Patience got on to Topper. It was lovely to be out "in company," and Jackie seemed to weigh just nothing, though I could feel that he was a bit anxious—we know a great deal more about our riders than they know about us. Poor little chap! Up till now his experiences had been unfortunate; they should be so no longer if I could help it. I had lost all my old nervousness; there was nothing for him to fear from sudden starts or shies, and as for my former lightness of heart which made me want to dance and gallop all the time, that was gone from me too. There was nothing for him to be afraid of. I could be depended on to do my very best.

He could rise nicely at the trot, but he could not sit down cantering yet; but that would soon come with practice.

He had the best of instructors in Patience. She was not only an excellent rider, but she knew what she was doing, and could explain things, which is not always the case with good riders. She insisted on long stirrups and long reins, and though it is always difficult to carry beginners, with their wobbly legs and queer, uncertain movements, I could feel that Jack was happy and that we were getting on very nicely. We were out about an hour, walking, trotting, and cantering, down one green lane, across some fields, and back by another.

"Hello, Jack!" said the Colonel, as he met us on our return. "How do you and Mousie get on together?"

"Oh, he's ever so easy to ride," said Jack. "I couldn't fall off him;

he's quite different from Queenie and Magpie."

The Colonel was delighted. He went in to fetch his wife, and they both came out to admire me.

"Well, Patience," said he, "you have done a good bit of work. A pony that will carry a boy like Jack nicely is worth his weight in gold; and if we can keep Mousie for him, no one will be more delighted than I shall be."

After this we went out every day for an hour or two.

Jack improved with his riding. He could sit down at the canter now, and was getting quite a good seat. I could feel that his nervousness was leaving him, and each day he enjoyed his rides more. He could also saddle me and bridle me without hurting my gums, and everybody was delighted.

Presently the day came when we were expecting Michael home for the holidays. How surprised he would be to see me and Jack! And we should all three go out for rides together! What fun we should have!

More exciting still, we were all to go to Exmoor for our summer holidays. This was news indeed. Nothing could have pleased Tinker and me more. We were going to a farm, right up on the moor. Tinker and I would visit Withypool Hill again; we would feel the springy, peaty ground beneath our feet, and crop the sweet heather and bog plants which only grow on our native heath; we would feel again the fresh wind that blew straight from the Severn Sea. To us there was no wind like it.

We could hear now a commotion in the hall—the drive was on the far side of the house. Michael must be home again. Yes, it was he sure enough, with his red head and happy face, and he had not been in the house a minute before he dashed out again to greet his Tinker, who was waiting for him with his head over the gate.

"And you," he said, as he turned to me, "why, it's the old Mousie back again! What has Patience been doing to you?"

I twitched my tail with the double twitch we Exmoors have, and stamped with delight, and Michael turned to Jack and said:

"As for Jack, I hear he has become a great horseman and means to cut his brother out altogether."

"I think I have improved," said Jack modestly.

"I should just think he has," said Patience; "he is getting on splendidly." We had a few good rides together before we started for Exmoor. I was amused to see Tinker sweating a bit and puffing up the steep hills. He had been doing no work, and was not in as good condition as Topper and me. I sometimes thought that he bucked a bit too much about himself—he had had such a very successful life—but he was a good sort all the same.

Next Sunday the Colonel was talking to the children in our field.

"You must understand," he said, "that if you take your ponies, you have got to look after them entirely yourselves. I cannot be bothered, and I want your mother to have a rest. You must see that their shoes are all right. All hind shoes must be removed for the journey, as the ponies will go together, and I don't want any accidents. Saddles and bridles must be in good repair, and you are to take your own cleaning things with you. We shall be a long way from a town, and it will be difficult to buy things. You are to box the ponies at 2.30 on Wednesday. The station-master will be ready for you. Mousie is the quietest, he will lead in first, and the others will follow. Your mother and I will be there a quarter of an hour later."

"Will the ponies be tied up?" said Jackie.

"No," said the Colonel; "they will be quite loose; small ponies travel much better that way. They will all three be together; the horse-boxes will have had their partitions taken out, and the ponies will be able to move about. Small ponies are not very safe tied up, because horse-boxes are made for horses and not ponies. They are much too big for ponies, and if a pony gets scared and plunges, anything may happen to him. The big horses have a couple of boxes ordered for them; they have both travelled before and will not, I hope, be nervous.

"When we arrive at Dulverton, Patience had better climb into the box and slip on the bridles and lead them out one by one. A strange porter might scare them; they are sure to be a bit upset. The saddles and bridles will travel in the coupé next to the box, and you must be careful to see that everything you put into the coupé is taken out again."

"Mayn't we travel in the coupé?" said Michael. "Murphy says he always does."

"We shall have to see what the station-master says," said the Colonel.

CHAPTER XX

The Exmoor Holiday—We Start in Good Order—Topper is Afraid—I Lead the Way into the Horse-Box—A Pleasant Journey ends in an Accident—The Motorist Who would not Stop—We Arrive at the Farm—A Lovely Stable—We Go for our First Ride—Back to Withypool.

THE great day arrived. Such a bustle there was in the morning, grooming, and cleaning, and packing. Jack kept tugging at my mane and tail with the comb until they were quite sore. How I wished that Patience was not so busy and would notice what he was at, and tell him to use the dandy-brush more and the comb less! However, there was something to make up. Jack was so much afraid that I would be hungry on the journey, that he kept on bringing me little supplies of oats, and this was very nice; but I had had a good feed at midday and soon began to feel rather uncomfortable. Perhaps it was just as well that Patience caught him at it.

"Oh, Jack," she said, quite annoyed for her, "for Heaven's sake don't do that! You will make him buck or bolt or something, and all the trouble I have taken will be wasted."

Jackie was penitent for the moment. It was an amiable trait in his character that he did so love to feed me up, and he could not be persuaded that any harm could come of it.

We started for the station in good time. Michael led the way on Tinker, and we went in single file, because it was a road where we expected to meet motors. Motorists seem to think that ponies are like motors, and have no nerves. I suppose they are so used to town life that they do not know how dreadfully nervous we are, and that it needs a well-broken, quiet pony to face the terrible traffic with its inconsiderate or ignorant drivers. What with nervousness, and the slipperiness, which makes a tarred road a terror to every horse and rider, Topper was sweating by the time we reached the station. He was only five and hadn't had much experience, and Patience had to soothe him and comfort him a good deal before he quieted down.

The station was nice and quiet, and the station-master had our horse-box ready for us. I walked in good as gold, with Topper at my tail, and

Tinker bringing up the rear. Patience stayed with us while the great door was closed and then she slipped our bridles and saddles off, and climbed out of the box—and there we were left in the dark.

Poor Topper! I was sorry for him. He was shaking and sweating with fear, and never stopped until we got out at Dulverton. He had never travelled before, and he was a nervous, high-strung pony, as most well-bred ponies are.

Tinker and I didn't worry; we knew all about it, and this journey was quite pleasant. The children had persuaded the station-master to let them travel in the coupé. How they did enjoy it! It was ever so much nicer than going in the ordinary carriage, and every few minutes they would open the little windows between them and us, and give us a handful of oats or a bit of something good. Topper couldn't touch a thing; he felt far too bad, but I did rather well myself. Well, after an hour or two, Jackie climbed up and looked through and called:

"Almost there, Mousie!"

"Only one more minute, Tinker!" said Michael.

"We're just arriving, Treasure!" said Patience to the trembling Topper. And then crash, bump, and at last a stop, and things got quieter.

Topper was in a cold sweat and quite assured the end of the world had come. However, all was now silent, and we could hear the children's voices, full of suppressed excitement, outside.

The big horses were got out first. They condescended to call to us, and of course we all called back.

"That's Mousie's voice!" cried Jackie, as I sent forth my deep call. Tinker's voice was high and shrill, and Topper's somewhere between the two. You couldn't mistake one for another, and of course the children knew our voices well. The top door was now opened, and Patience talked to us quietly. She climbed over, and quickly had our bridles on. Then the great door was dropped down with a clatter and bang, and out we came. The children put our saddles on, and we were led off to the "Carnarvon Arms," near the station. Here we were to have a drink and a mouthful of hay, while the children had tea, and then we were to start off for Shervage Farm, nine miles all along the River Barle.

What fun it was!

First went Mrs. Coke on her wise old hunter, then the Colonel, and then came the ponies. We felt so proud to be going all together and with such big horses.

"Be careful!" said Colonel Coke, as we left the yard. "There is a nasty bit of tarred road on the way to Dulverton, and I am afraid the motors are bad."

The road was horrid. I felt thankful that I had had so much practice in keeping my feet. And of course the selfishness or the ignorance—I never could tell which it was—of the motor-drivers made it worse.

Topper came just behind me, and I could hear his feet slipping every now and then, and I knew that he was very nervous by the way Patience was trying to reassure him as the motors flew past, each one seeming more noisy and to come closer to us than the one before. We had gone only half a mile when we saw two motors ahead of us. They were coming very fast and one was trying to overtake the other. The Colonel held up his hand to warn them of danger, but they took no notice, and just as they were passing Topper, the one behind tried to push past the other. This brought him within a yard of Topper. The pony made up his mind the horrible beast was coming straight for him. He began to prance with fear. There was a loud slithering noise. He had no footing on that slippery road, and he was down.

Patience was shot half across the road. She was badly shaken and bruised, and terribly upset about her pony. Topper had fallen on his side, and was on his legs again almost at once, terrified and shaken.

The motorist had pulled up a few yards ahead, and came back to find out what damage was done. Seeing Patience and Topper both on their legs he seemed quite reassured, and went off, saying he was glad no harm had been done.

"You are mistaken," said the Colonel sharply. "It is impossible to tell with a pony or a horse how much harm has been done until you find out how much he has been frightened."

The man looked sulky and went off, obviously thinking he had been hardly used, but the Colonel was perfectly right. Topper had been thoroughly scared, and it needed months of careful riding on the part of his mistress before he could be considered quiet with motors again.

Patience did not mind her bruises or the scratches Topper had received, but she minded very much about this; she realized fully that it is a very long time before a horse who gets a bad fright is reliable again. Murphy was always saying: "Never let a horse get a bad fright if you can help it. He may never get over it."

We were a chastened party as we turned off from the dangers of the road to the enchanting little path that runs up and down through the old oak woods just above the River Barle. What a lovely river it is! Here a quiet brown pool, under a steep overhanging bank; there, dancing and gurgling in the sunlight, and then a mass of dark green moss-covered boulders stretching right across.

Here we soon cheered up. Ponies love these up-and-down paths, and we hoped we should not see another motor for a long long time. Up and down we followed the course of the river, getting a little higher every mile. How good it all smelt! And no one enjoyed it so much as Tinker and I; we felt we were in our own country now. A few miles more and we should be on the heather.

Yes, here we were at last, a steep up hill, Gurt Gate, and the heather of Shervage under our feet.

All was ready at our farm. One field for the ponies, and another for the horses beside it.

The children offered us a drink, slipped off our saddles and bridles, and dried our backs; and then we had a good roll in our field, and settled down to enjoy ourselves, while they went in to an early supper. Topper was himself again.

"Why can't all the world be like this?" he said—and it was many years before he forgot what he always alluded to as "the slippery road and the savage motor." He was firmly convinced that that motor had had every intention of eating him if Providence had not intervened. "It came straight for me, roaring," he used to say.

Later in the evening the three children came to see how we were, each bringing with them a wooden box. They placed these in a row, far enough to be well out of kicking distance, and in them they put a feed of oats for each of us.

"We must feed them well up now," said Jack with satisfaction, "because they have got to do a lot of work."

We thoroughly enjoyed our dinner, and had a restful night under the quiet stars. It was much cooler up on Exmoor than down in the lowlands, and before many weeks had passed we found that we were better moving about and grazing at night, and getting our sleep when the sun rose and we could pick out a slope where its rays warmed us.

The next morning the children came for us at 9 o'clock; they brought our halters with them and led us off to the stable. There within, we saw the big horses already hard at work on their morning feed. There were only two empty stalls left. Topper was put in one and Tinker and I shared the other.

"Exmoors are such gentlemen," said Patience; "they won't go nabbing and kicking at each other like other horses would."

We had another lovely meal. The children watched us the whole time, making flattering remarks about our wonderful "points" and virtues, and then we were left for an hour to digest. It was cool and peaceful and homely in that stable. Not nearly as grand as ours at home—and a lot of smart grooms would have turned up their noses at it—but it was just the sort of place one could rest in, have a quiet nap, and happy dreams. All stables are not like that, and some that their owners think very grand are the least homely to us ponies.

In an hour the children were back again. Mrs. Coke was with them and looking round, saying:

"We must find room somewhere in the stable for the saddles; we can't keep five saddles in our sitting-room, but every peg here seems crowded."

The farmer came in at that moment and soon solved the trouble.

"I'll soon put you up pegs for the saddle and bridles, M'am," he said. "There'll be plenty of room next door if you don't mind getting them from there; and the Colonel said he'd like some wooden balls too, to weight the halter ropes. I'll make you some of those."

"How different from townsfolk!" said Mrs. Coke. "They expect to have everything done for them, and don't seem able to make anything for themselves—people in the country are much more independent."

We were soon ready, saddles and bridles on, and off we started. We never went out at home all together like this, and it really was very exciting, and of course we ponies were bent on showing that we were faster and more capable in every way than the horses.

The children had got their sandwiches, and we were to be out for lunch.

"I think we must go up the Barle our first day," said the Colonel. "We will ride as far as Withypool, and then strike up on to Winsford Hill, and back again by Tarr Steps."

Tinker and I pricked up our ears. Supposing we should meet My Mother and Aunt, how exciting that would be! But we never saw them all the time that we were on Exmoor.

It was lovely by the Barle; we forded the river at Tarr Steps, where it was shallow. Topper started pawing half-way across, he had thoughts of lying down. He wasn't used to fording rivers, and didn't quite know how to behave himself, and Patience had to give him a good whack before he would go on. The turf was perfect, short, springy grass; it never gets too dry on Exmoor; and then we came to woods of little ancient oaks, and delicious paths winding up and down, in and out, but keeping close to the river all the time. They were so narrow that often we could only go in single file, but in places they would broaden out again, and we could go two or three abreast.

Then our path crossed the river once more; a very deep place this, and Topper was a bit nervous, which made Tinker and me smile. He hadn't been brought up by the Barle as we had. Tinker and I had forded it a hundred times following My Mother and Aunt. Another mile or two of open greensward and little woods full of ferns and stunted oak trees, some of them wreathed with honeysuckle, and we reached a pleasant, open, grassy space all surrounded with trees—"just the sort of place to meet Robin Hood," said Jack; and here Mrs. Coke called a halt and announced that it was lunch time.

"Be careful how you tie the ponies up," said the Colonel. "They must not be able to kick each other, and the branch must have some 'give' in it; and you must use the tie I taught you, or we shall be having broken reins and lost ponies."

La Cavale la vue au milieu des mères

They found a pleasant shady place for us, where we were tied to the branches of an old beech hedge. How beautiful it all was! And then they went off to lie in the bracken beyond and eat their lunch. We were very happy—taking a bite of green beech, then a tuft of heather, or a mouthful of fern; such a variety of delicious delicacies—it was most enjoyable. Tinker and I were in our element; it was home to us—the place we were reared in, and that to most of us is the place that will always remain nearest to our hearts.

Half an hour's rest and we were ready to go on. The children tightened our girths and mounted. We crossed the river once more, climbed up the hill through the old beech trees, and saw Withypool below us.

Tinker and I stared. Well we remembered Withypool, and better still the hill beyond it, where we were born. Today, however, we were to go nearer to our birthplace: we turned right-handed and went over the top of Winsford Hill. Here we had another laugh at Topper; he saw what he considered a nice bit of turf—"any pony of intelligence," said Tinker, "would have known that it was bog"—and he very nearly went into it, but was just warned in time. It was lovely up here, so fresh and airy. We cantered and trotted along the grassy ways, with heather on either side of us, going a good pace; and soon we were going down again to Tarr Steps. We crossed the Barle, trotted through the fir wood, and then mounted that very steep hill for home.

We were none of us in good condition yet, and there was a good deal of puffing and blowing up that hill; though in a fortnight's time we should be thinking nothing of it.

"The ponies are hot," said the Colonel, when we reached the top. "You had better get off and loosen their girths, and lead them home, it is only five minutes' walk. We must be a bit careful of them until they get into condition; and be sure to dry their backs when you get in, you cannot take too much care the first week."

We soon reached the farm, and there were the farmer and his wife waiting to welcome us. They were so interested in us all, and specially in Tinker and me. We soon found that to be an Exmoor pony on Exmoor was the shortest road to everybody's interest and affection.

"You'll be wanting your tea now, young gentlemen," said Mrs. Hobbs, "you didn't take much in the way of dinner."

"I'm just longing for my tea," said Jack, "and some more of your lovely butter and Devonshire cream; we don't get that at home."

They took us into the yard, unsaddled us, and gave us a good rub where our backs were wet from the saddle, with a handful of straw, and then we were turned out in our peaceful field. We had a glorious roll over and over—the grass was delicious; and then later in the evening they brought us out another feed of oats.

"And tomorrow," said Patience, "you are to have a rest, and the next day we will go for another lovely ride."

That was good news. We were not tired, but being out of condition, a quiet day would be very acceptable, and then we would enjoy our next ride all the more. This was the right sort of life for a pony.

"And I shall be stiff tomorrow, I expect," said Jack. "We were out four hours, the longest ride I've ever had."

CHAPTER XXI

Jack Goes for His First Ride Alone—The Song of the Danish Boy—We See Salmon in the River—Michael and Patience go Stag-hunting—Michael is Safe with Tinker—Tinker's Fine Exploit—I Long to go Hunting Too—Tinker Fords the Flooded River—I Long to Prove Myself as Good as Tinker Bell.

JACK got on with his riding well. These long steady rides were just what he needed to give him a good seat. He got well down in his saddle, and began to look quite at home. We had been at Shervage just a month when Jack was allowed to go out for his first ride alone. He and I thoroughly enjoyed ourselves. Jack kept talking to me—horses like that—and I put first one ear back and then another, to hear what he was saying. Once or twice he got off to pick himself some whortleberries or wild raspberries, and he always found something extra nice to give me. We went right down to the Danesbrook, through what Jack called the Fairy Wood, and followed the stream down until it reached the Barle; and there we turned back towards home.

There were mossy tree trunks lying across the path on the ground, and Jack was longing to jump them; but he did not feel quite sure he could stick on, so we went round them instead.

Some of the time he sang to me.

"I have learnt a song on purpose for you, Mousie," he said. "It is about a little Danish boy who got left behind with the Ancient Britons, and he was very lonely without his own people. They didn't understand him, but the animals did, and they were very fond of him. He lived on the Quantock Hills, over away on the right, where you and I will go one day.

"The song goes like this:

> " 'Of flocks upon the neighbouring hills
> He is the darling and the joy,
> And often when no cause appears,
> The mountain ponies prick their ears
> -They hear the Danish boy-

  While in his dell he sings alone
  Beside the tree and corner-stone.' "

Jackie sang it to a tune of his own, and I thought it was very pretty. How often I had seen the ponies prick their ears like that; now I should know that perhaps they were listening to their friend the Danish boy.

We came now to a grassy glade with great oak trees on one hand rising up the hill-side, and the river with its huge mossy stones on our right. Jack got off and hitched my reins over the branch of a nut tree.

"I'm going to peep and see whether there are any salmon in the big pool today," he said. And there, sure enough, he spied two huge fellows swimming lazily round and round one after the other. Jack watched them for some time. "Michael will be cross," he said, "that he has missed that."

But Michael was having great fun on his own account, and when we got home we heard about it. He and Patience had gone off together hoping to meet the staghounds. They had met at North Molton, and the children, taking the advice of Mr. Hobbs, had gone out to Willingford Bridge hoping to meet them and get a run. Sure enough about midday they heard the baying of the great hounds coming on their right; they did not see the stag, but the hounds seemed to have a good line. They were running, strung out one after the other in single file, not coming on all together so that a sheet might cover them—as fox-hunting people say— but they were going a good pace, ever so much faster than they looked. The Field following them was not very big, it was still early in the season. The children kept their ponies back until most of the Field had passed and then they let them go. They had a glorious gallop! Right over Molland Moor, then down through Lyshwells, over the Danesbrook, then right along where Jack and I had been that very morning. Then they came to the Barle again, crossed it, and up over Winsford Hill. When they started to go down near Winsford village, Patience thought Topper had had enough; she didn't want to tire him, or overexcite him. Topper was still young, and not in hard condition, and the run promised to be a long one, so she turned home and was back about 4 o'clock. But Michael never came for hours after. Nobody was really anxious about him, because they knew what a wonderful pony Tinker was.

"I don't think anything is at all likely to go wrong with that pony," the Colonel said to his wife. "If Michael was on Topper it would be a different thing. Topper has got a lot to learn, but an Exmoor pony would never make a mistake on the moor, and Tinker is so well-mannered and never gets overexcited."

At about 6 o'clock a neighbouring farmer turned in to give us news.

"We have had a good run," he said; "killed at Chetsford Water. Your young gentleman went first class; he was enjoying himself no end, and the pony too; but he seemed to think that the pony was tired coming home, and when we passed Exford he got off to walk. Pony looked right enough—an Exmoor pony is never tired—but there was no persuading your young man, and I thought I'd step in and tell you that he's all right and will be back soon. Proper little sportsman he is!"

Sure enough Michael turned up in another hour. Tinker came trotting in beside him; he had walked the best part of six miles. Tinker was quite indignant.

"Couldn't persuade him to get on," he said.

"Never mind," said the big hunters, "it's a fault on the right side. Michael is the right sort, he thinks of his pony before himself!"

Michael came out several times that evening to see Tinker. He was still anxious about him; he could not believe that after that splendid run—such a pace and covering so much country—Tinker was not tired.

He himself was very excited, and it was a long time before he got to sleep that night. He had thoroughly enjoyed himself. It was the best run he had ever had, and he had never enjoyed anything so much in his life; and Tinker had been so wonderful, kept on galloping in the most marvellous way, and the only pony who was in at the death!

How I wished that Jack and I had been there too! But Jack was not yet quite experienced enough to go hunting. However, wait a bit, I thought, and we will show them!

After this Michael was always thinking about hunting. Whenever we were out he would keep listening, hoping to hear the voices of the big hounds coming over the hill.

Dann in stiller Jugend wird's die Wärme

Before we went home again he and Tinker had another very exciting experience. They were down near the Barle, quite near Bradley Ham, when they heard the hounds coming. They followed their deer down to the Barle and ran along the left bank towards Tarr Steps. Some of the Field crossed the river, thinking there was better going on the right side, and Michael and Tinker went with them.

They galloped down the river at a great pace, and after a mile or two they came to the deep crossing. Now Michael had been this way several times, and he knew exactly how the ford went. It did not cross the river at right angles, but the exit was some yards below where one would have expected to find it. The river was very full after heavy rains the night before, and Michael would not have tried to venture across, had there not been a good reason for it. The riders wanted to cross badly. They knew there was a ford, but exactly how it went nobody there knew except Michael.

"It may be too deep for Tinker," he said to himself, "but I know he can swim, and the current is not too strong for him. Hobbs says the Exmoors often swim the river when it is flooded."

One man was trying to persuade a big thoroughbred horse to enter the water. The horse kept rearing right up, but he was afraid to go in.

Michael and Tinker slipped down the little path and into the water. It got deep very suddenly and Tinker was all but swimming. "My tail streamed out quite level with my back," he told us afterwards, "and I was right up on the tips of my toes."

Michael thoroughly enjoyed this, though he could not keep his legs dry, tuck them up high as he would. A few seconds and they emerged dripping the other side.

The other riders followed. One excitable nervous horse slipped down, and he and his rider got a thorough ducking. Meanwhile Michael and Tinker were galloping as hard as they could go for Tarr steps—well pleased with themselves, as they deserved to be—and there the hounds killed; and of course, after this adventure Michael was keener than ever. Patience did not care about hunting quite as much. She was a much quieter nature, and she loved to ride out and look at all the beautiful country, and train Topper to be a first-class pony, as indeed he was rapidly becoming.

The heather had come and gone. First with its honey-scent heavy in the air, and the bees tumbling over each other in ecstasy; and later scattering clouds of dusty pollen wherever we stepped. Instead of miles of purple heather, the great rolling hill-sides were turning shades of gold and russet wherever the bracken grew. The whortleberry pickers had been busy gathering their annual harvest, popping up unexpectedly below our noses. One had given Tinker such a start that he shied Michael off, but he fell comfortably into a tussock of heather—"quite the best fall I have ever had," he said as he picked himself up. It was now September, and time to be off home again.

We were all very sad at leaving the farmer and his wife. How kind they had been to us! We should never forget them, and we hoped to come back again and see them next year; that was something to look forward to.

And then we had to say good-bye to the dogs and the cats, the chickens and the ducks, the cows and the horses and the pigs. What fun we had all had together!

But it was time to go; the children had to be packed off to school next week.

We had had a lovely holiday. I felt years younger. I could not have believed that a holiday in my native air would have made me feel so young, so different!

"Mousie's getting his old self again," said the Colonel one day, as he noticed me with my mouth open, chivvying a cheeky heifer down the field. I should not have dreamed six months ago that I should ever do that sort of thing again, and be able to enjoy it.

CHAPTER XXII

We Return to Wootten—Jack Learns to Jump—Michael goes Hunting—He Brags a Little—Michael Wins a Brush—Jack Longs to Do So as Well—So Do I—Tinker Bell is Discouraging—I Make Up My Mind that Jack Shall get a Brush!—Jack Hunts for the First Time.

HAPPY as we were on Exmoor, it was very exciting to be home again. There was so much to see and to find out. The grass had grown tremendously: no stock had been in our field since we left. No fear of a shortage this winter. And our lovely great elm trees were turning pale gold in great patches. Everything was the same and yet changed. Patience and Michael went off to school at the end of the week. Patience gave Jack all sorts of instructions about me before she left.

"Get on with your riding," she said, "and I shouldn't wonder if you and I don't get some hunting in the Christmas holidays; and be sure not to forget Topper's lump of sugar on Sundays."

It seemed lonely after they went away, but we got used to it in time. Jack took me out most days. Sometimes we went with the Colonel and sometimes Jack was allowed to go alone. He was becoming a good little horseman, and getting quite hopeful that he might be allowed to go out hunting at Christmas.

"You must learn to jump first," said the Colonel. "We shall have to leave that to Patience; she's a first-class teacher, and when you can jump two feet, without interfering with your pony's mouth, keeping your legs steady and your hands down, you shall go out with the hounds."

We ponies had tremendous long shaggy coats by now, and we needed them. There was a lot of rain and wind that autumn, and the shed was no good to us; we never cared to shelter there, we always had a feeling that it was safer in the open. But the time passed very quickly, and the Christmas holidays were soon here.

A sound of the motor in the drive; excited voices in the hall; and almost at once Patience and Michael scrambling over the railings to hug each their own pony. Topper and Tinker were delighted! Directly they heard those voices they had flung up their heads to listen, and so soon as they spied the children they trotted up to the rails, making their soft love call through their nostrils. "The biggest compliment a horse can pay you," I heard Murphy say once.

Jack and I were not going to be out of all this love-making. I went up to him and laid my head on his shoulder, and he stroked my nose.

"Well, Jack, how's your riding getting on?" said Michael. "Can you jump yet?"

"No! But I'm to start learning at once, now Patience is back, and Father says I'll get on quick now, 'cos I'm ready for it, and directly I can jump two feet without shifting I may go hunting."

"Two feet!" said Michael. "Why, you'll have to jump six out hunting."

"Nonsense!" said Patience. "If he can jump two in good style in cold blood, he can jump anything out hunting when Mousie gets going; it's ever so much easier, and the jumps aren't a bit difficult out hunting really."

The very next day we began. The children spent the morning building up what they called the steeple-chase course, in Long Acre. First there was a tiny jump of faggots, very low, but just so that it was easier to jump than to walk over. Then came two posts and a rail that slipped down if you hit it hard, and last, a little stand-up fence made of furze. They were all quite low and most inviting, just about forty yards apart.

In the afternoon Patience and Jack came out for Jack's first lesson. Patience rode me first over these little fences, so as to make sure I understood. She was getting heavier now, but she rode so well that her weight was nothing. She held me just right, so that jumping was the easiest thing in the world. She did not hang on to the reins as we landed, nor did she come down plop on my loins after every jump, as so many riders do.

We went over the course two or three times very slowly, and then Jack got on, and Patience mounted Topper.

"I want you to start when I do," she said, "and jump alongside. I am going to the right, you go to the left. Try and go slow, not out of a trot, if you can manage it—and we will pull up when we get over. All you have got to do is keep his head straight and tip your shoulders forward as he rises, and you will find yourself on the other side."

Off went Patience and Topper at a steady canter. Topper, being nearly thoroughbred, hated trotting, and close after and a little to the left came Jack and me. I rose easily, felt Jack shift a bit backwards, but not much, come down with a flop, and that was his first real jump. We pulled up, and they gave us a lump of sugar and patted us. Then we went back for another try.

"Don't hurry, Jack," said Patience, "you can't be too slow jumping, or your pony may get upset and take a dislike to it. It's really quite easy, you've only got to get in time with him. It needs practice, that's all."

Well, we tried about twenty times, with varying success, but Jack enjoyed himself. There was nothing to make him nervous, he really could not have fallen off.

We did this every day for a week. Every time we came over that fence, Jack left the saddle a little and came down flop; fortunately he was a light weight, and so this did not hurt me.

"I don't think I shall ever be able to jump a hurdle," he said one day.

"Indeed you will!" said Patience. "It'll come all of a sudden. It did with me. You've just got to get your time right, that's all. Try leaning a little more forward as Mousie takes off, and then you won't get 'left behind.' " This was most successful, and we had two or three really good jumps.

"Next week we'll do the whole course," said Patience. "I think really you'll find it easier. This starting and stopping always makes things more difficult."

On Monday we had a splendid day.

"We'll do the whole course," said Patience. "Call out if you want to stop, otherwise I shall go ahead; and remember about tipping your body forward."

Jack arrived at the end, radiant.

"It really is easier," he said, "going straight ahead. I did one beautifully, the other two were just middling."

"You'll soon get on," said Patience. "We'll give the parents a show at the end of the week."

And so they did. Jack jumped two of the three fences in perfect style,

His first real jump

and was now certified as being ready to go hunting.

Twice a week Michael had been out with the foxhounds, and every day brought back glowing tales. After hunting his tongue never stopped: what the Master said; how Tom the Whip got his fall; Miss X.'s new horse; how Farmer J. showed them the short way, and smashed the big rails; the brook that only two of the Field tackled; how young Y. jumped the boundary fence; and Tinker's jump, Tinker's huge, marvellous jump over that big rail at Park End.

"And what about the hounds?" the Colonel would say. "Did you happen to notice what they were doing? It seems to me, young man, that you're a bit too keen on galloping and jumping to notice anything else!"

And then one day a most exciting thing happened. Michael came home almost beside himself with pride and joy; and since he had been going to a real big school—a public school I heard his father call it once—he had taken great pains to look as though he was much too old and wise to get really wildly excited about anything. He mother was gardening in the grounds just close to our paddock, and he rushed up to her shouting:

"Look, Mother! What do you think? I've got the brush! They gave it me because, though there were a lot of grown-up people at the kill, I was the youngest. Isn't it splendid!"

"Splendid, my dear! I *am* proud," said his mother. "Tinker must have gone well!"

"Rather—and I handled him jolly well too." Michael was sometimes just a little inclined to brag these holidays. "You should have seen me putting him to that high bank down at the bottom of Lee's coppice."

Colonel Coke, Patience, and Jack came out then, and had to be told the story all over again.

"Even Patience has never got the brush yet," said Michael.

His father looked at him and raised his eyebrows. "Patience wasn't out today—if she had been, yours wouldn't have been the only pony up at the kill perhaps," he said.

Michael looked a little bit ashamed.

"Oh, I would love to get a brush some day," said Jack. "I don't suppose I'll ever ride well enough."

"Well, perhaps you will later on, when you've got a new pony."

"Oh, Michael!" said Patience.

Michael meant to be kind to his little brother, of course, but he didn't consider me leaning over the fence and listening with all my ears, and how dreadfully sad it was to know that nobody thought me good enough any longer to do what Tinker Bell could.

Tinker himself took the same tone later.

"It isn't likely, Mousie, my dear, after the hard times you've had. I'm sure you're wonderful as it is, but it takes a bit of doing to be in at the death."

I was so unhappy that I could hardly eat my oats, and then it came into my mind that I had improved so much already that I might still do more; and what but that did dear Patience mean when she said, "Oh, Michael!" in that gentle, hurt voice? From that day I resolved that if, by behaving myself well and doing my best, and never caring if I were tired or hungry, and never letting myself flinch if I was afraid, I could get a brush for Jack, and prove that he and I were as good as Michael and Tinker, I would do it.

Next week Michael was to go away to stay with some cousins.

"They don't even ride," said Michael. "They go along the roads at fifty miles an hour, risking other people's lives, and they call that sport; and in the evening they go to dances and cinemas."

"They say they can't afford ponies," said Patience.

"That's no excuse," answered Michael. "Father says our ponies never cost him more than five shillings a week."

"We shan't be able to afford stabled horses, anyway, when we grow up," said Jack, "until we can make some money."

"All the more important to make the most of the ponies now," said Michael. "I wish I wasn't the eldest. Next time the cousins want one of us you'll have to go, Jack."

But there was no escape for Michael.

"You must learn to get on with all sorts of people," said the Colonel. "It's very kind of them to ask you."

Jack had his first hunt that week. How excited he was—but not so excited as I was! He went with Patience, and thoroughly enjoyed himself. Our first day was a very quiet one—no chance of being in the first flight, for Patience was beginning gently with him, in her usual wise way—but Jack found it full of thrills. To ride through those glorious woods, into which he had peered, but had never been allowed to go; to canter along that grassy footpath up to Old Farm; really to see at last that romantic house near Oldbury, of which he had heard many tales, though he had never yet been allowed further than the big gates—that alone was exciting. But there were all those glorious horses too, and horses, not standing still, but moving, changing every moment—browns, bays, chestnuts, long tails, short tails, fifteen hands and over, and little ponies no bigger than me.

And then there was the Field. Nearly everyone had a word or a smile for Jack, and as for the farmers who were there, no one out hunting could have been more delightful, more kind, or more humorous; they were always ready to help the children, nothing ever seemed a trouble to them.

The hounds were splendid too, white and dappled bodies with long sterns waving, slipping through the grey trunks and thick brushwood, the sun glinting on their bright beautiful sides; a touch of pink as the huntsman followed them on his big horse, with his cheery voice, and the occasional toot of his horn—that made up a picture that could not be equalled anywhere.

Jack came back in raptures.

"Never, never have I had such a day," he said. After this we went out once or twice a week whenever the hounds met near.

He made progress each day. I could feel him getting more down in his saddle, and firmer in his seat. He got more at home each week in the hunting-field, and less overexcited. Sometimes, when we had gone well, I dreamed that we really had got a brush, and proved ourselves as good as others. Michael was home again, and hunting regularly with his father. They went with a different pack which met rather further off.

"He is much better hunting with me," said the Colonel to his wife. "He is a bit too wild, and he might upset Jack's pony, and then everything would go wrong. Patience is quite first class. She is never in a hurry, and never gets overexcited; she has just the right temperament for dealing with horses, and I have more confidence in her for getting

Jack on with his riding than anybody. In fact, we owe a great deal to her, and so does Mousie; she has been the making of him; it is an achievement."

CHAPTER XXIII

The Last Meet of the Season—Can We be in at the Death?—My Great Ambition—The Run—Jack's Fine Riding—The Difficult Jump—The Kill—The Master says, "Well done, children!"—Jack Gets the Mask—Our Triumphant Return—Tinker Turns Out a Trump—"A Mask's as good as a Brush Any Day"—Good-night, Pony, King of the Ponies!"

THE Christmas holidays had been a busy time, but they were coming to an end now. Tomorrow would be our last hunting day; it was now for that brush or never till next season, for the week after would see all the children back at school. It was to be Jack's first term.

I was feeling strong and fit. I was having an extra feed of oats each day. I was full of muscle, and never seemed to tire. Mrs. Coke did not approve of a long day's hunting for children, and the orders were that we should turn homewards at 2 o'clock unless hounds were running, when we could stay out a bit longer.

Jack was turning out a splendid little rider; of course he had Patience to coach him, and that was a great help; but I think he had inherited a gift for riding—he sat so well, and it seemed natural to him to ride with long reins, and, best of all, he had lost all his nervousness. I was thinking over all this, as I digested my evening feed, when the children came back to see whether we had finished up our dinners clean.

They were talking hard, and seemed very excited.

"What time do we start?" said Jack. "It's only six miles," said Patience. "Ten o'clock will do us nicely, and of course it's the best meet we have. Be sure not to forget what I told you, Jack: if he's fidgety at the meet, keep him walking about. I'll come with you, and when they find, you follow me, and don't get excited."

At 8 o'clock next morning the children took us into the stable and gave us a good feed before they went in to their own breakfast.

"They must have time to digest," said Patience, "or their oats will do them no good."

At 9.30 they were back to saddle and bridle us, and at 10 sharp we were off.

The day was perfect, bright and cloudy, and we were all four well

116

content as we jogged along steadily at six miles an hour, through the green lanes and across the fields. Patience had a wonderful eye for country; she always knew the shortest ways, and seldom forgot a way that she had once been. She was, too, such a favourite with the farmers that she was allowed to take lots of short cuts across their land. In fact, we hardly touched a tarred road the whole time. "Such a comfort," said Jack, and we thought so too.

The meet was a small one, not more than forty altogether. I felt so strong and well that I couldn't stand quite still; but Jack walked me round and round, so that I gradually got quieter, and when the Master, who was hunting hounds himself today, trotted off for the nearest covert, Topper and I fell in sedately in the rear. "The proper place for children's ponies," Colonel Coke always said.

Well, nothing particular happened for a long time, but the woods were so beautiful that nobody cared except me. Stepping along softly over the dark green moss, between the great fir trees; splashing through the streams at the bottom; and trotting gaily through half a dozen fields until we came to Oak Tree Wood, with its deep rides—all this was joy enough for most riders and their horses.

Then suddenly they found.

First one whimper, then another, then half a dozen together. The sharp twang of the Master's horn, the Whip galloping hard down the ride, and we were off!

"Steady, Jack!" said Patience. But there wasn't much steady about Patience, we thought. Her blue eyes were alight, her pink cheeks blazing, her pig-tails flying, and it was all we could do to keep up with her. What a pace Topper could go! Down one ride we galloped, up another, and away right-handed through the big woodlands. The branches were low in places, and we ponies had a great advantage there; the big horses many a time had to slacken their pace to save their riders' faces.

"There's a big tree trunk to jump," called Patience suddenly. "Shall we go round?"

"No!" shouted Jack; it was the first word he had spoken since we started. Topper gave us a splendid lead, and Jack and I flew over

117

without the slightest jar.

"Well done!" called Patience; and I could feel Jack warming to his work. His blood was up now, and he would take a lot of stopping. I could feel his little knees grip the saddle as he stood in his stirrups to ease my back.

Now we had come to the end of the big woods; open fields were ahead of us, and we should have to be careful or we should get left. First came an open gate, then a big field with no exit except over a bank—a big place, but nothing to an Exmoor Pony, and, between you and me, we managed it considerably better than Topper, who never could really understand banks. What he liked was a clean jump, like rails. Then we caught up with the Field—they had been pulled up by a stiff bit of timber. There were four slip rails, and someone was pulling down the top one. The Master jumped it, and half a dozen of the Field; and then someone jumped off and pulled out another rail. Now I could jump it easily, I knew. Topper was eager to go for it. A kindly farmer called out:

"It's too much for those ponies. I'll pull out another rail."

"No, thank you," called Patience, and flew over it like a bird, and I after her. Another field and then an awkward gap. One man got his hat smashed by an overhanging bough; another had his knee bruised against a tree; but it is at this sort of place that we mountain ponies shine. "Clever as cats," Murphy often said. Topper, even though he was such a galloping sort, and not good at cramped places, did it beautifully, but that was mainly because Patience had such good hands.

Then came a very trappy place, not at all the place for big horses unless they were handy. The Whip took a toss on the far side; most of the Field didn't like the look of this, and they galloped off to find a better place. Patience, who never let this sort of thing fluster her, judged that the place was all right for people who had their ponies well in hand. We had to jump first on to the top of a high bank, then walk half a dozen yards along the top between beech stems, then spring off over a rather wide ditch into the field beyond. It was at this last place that the Whip had fallen, but he was up now and half across the next field. I think the bank was a bit rotten, and his horse had failed to get good foothold as he

They had killed at the bottom

took off. Topper went first, and I followed. It was child's play to me, a mere nothing; and as we landed in the far field, we realised joyfully that hounds were still streaming away on our right, and only the Master, the Whip, and ourselves were with them.

"Hooroosh!" shouted Jack, as we fled down hill. How my heart thumped with excitement! Was I going to prove myself as good as Tinker after all, as good as Patience deserved that I should be—which mattered more—and make my little master proud of me?

The field ended in a lane, narrowing to a path as steep as the side of a house. We pulled back to a walk, slipping and sliding on our haunches. A renewed outburst from the hounds, a twang from the Master's horn, and then silence. They had killed at the bottom. There they all were, the pied beauties, all their sterns going, and their great liquid speaking eyes asking for approval. And nobody there but the Master, the Whip, and Topper and Patience, Jack and me!

"Well done, children!" said the Master. "Did you enjoy your ride? You've got a couple of good ponies! There's a brush for Patience, and a mask for Master Jack. The Whip'll bring it round tomorrow, I dare say, but I thought, young man, that I was told in the summer that you were a bit nervous out riding. It doesn't look like it!"

"Oh, I couldn't be nervous with this pony," said Jack. "I couldn't fall off him."

The Field came up then, and the children turned homewards. Patience had tied the brush to the front of her saddle, and the Whip had promised to bring Jack's mask next day.

They had eight miles to go, and it was 3 o'clock. Mrs. Coke would be getting anxious, but Patience, having that invaluable "eye for country," and knowing every short cut and lane, would soon get us home again. How happy I was! How happy and proud I felt, that I could have trotted to the world's end and jumped the moon for sheer happiness!

At the first steep hill they got off, loosened our girths, and gave us a drink at the stream at the bottom and a mouthful of grass, while they ate their biscuits, for which there had been no time before.

Jack was all for walking. He thought I must be tired. But I was not a bit tired, and it was not until I had butted him repeatedly in the back with my head, that I persuaded him to mount, and we jogged on again.

Four-thirty—and there were the stable gates.

"Hulloa, darlings!" called Mrs. Coke. "I was getting anxious about you."

"We've had the time of our lives," said the children. "We've had a glorious run. Look what we have got, and Jack's mask is coming tomorrow!"

"Well done!" said Mrs. Coke. "I am proud of you all. Well done, old Mousie!" Her kind hand patted my neck. "Bring the ponies in. I have got a bran-mash ready, and I'll turn them out the minute they've finished, and we'll give them a feed this evening. You run in and have your hot baths; order your poached eggs as you go in. Can you be down to tea in a quarter of an hour?"

We enjoyed our mash—lots of oats with it, and a little hay to top up with. And then, before we had time to stand and get chilly, Mrs. Coke turned us out into our lovely field, where we had a good roll and shook ourselves, until we felt our coats comfortable again.

How I enjoyed telling Tinker Bell all about it! I tried not to brag, and he was splendid.

"A mask's as good as a brush any day. You've come back into the top class, and no mistake," he said. I pretended to bite his ear, just fondling it between my lips, because I was too happy to go on talking.

At seven o'clock, when it was quite dark, we heard the children coming with our evening feed—oats, and bran, and chaff.

They were still talking, very excited, and going over in memory every field and every jump.

"Good-night, ponies darling," said Patience, "sleep well." And Jackie kissed me on my neck, just up behind my ear, and whispered, "Good-night, pony, King of the Ponies!"